The Bottom of This...

By Tramaine Hannah

Scripture taken from the HOLY BIBLE, NEW INTERNATIONAL VERSION®. NIV®. Copyright © 1973, 1978, 1984 by International Bible Society. Used by permission of Zondervan. All rights reserved worldwide.

Higher Ground Books & Media
Springfield, Ohio.
http://highergroundbooksandmedia.com

Printed in the United States of America 2020

Looking Back

Nattalie stood in the center of her bedroom trembling from head to toe. Tears streaming down her bruised caramel cheeks and over her bleeding lips. Beads of sweat began to form on her brow as she listened to the sound of approaching footsteps on the hardwood floors. She tried to think of a way to get out of that room but there was no way around him. Drawing in a deep breath she grabbed hold of a pair of scissors on her dresser.

"Don't you come another step!" she shouted. Anderson glared at Nattalie. His fists were tight, and his chest heaved up and down, appearing to almost burst through his shirt. He began to walk towards her. "I said STOP!" She began to sob as she found herself backed against her dresser. Anderson placed one hand on his hip and with the other began to rub his forehead. He closed his eyes briefly. "Why would you want to hurt me Nattie? Why? When I love you so much? We belong together and nothing else matters!" Tears welled up in his eyes as he slowly moved in her direction. The desperation that oozed from his stare was enough to put her stomach in knots. She knew that stare. He wanted her. He needed her. She was no less important than the blood that flowed through his veins and he would never give her up. Anderson began to open his arms to her.

"Nattie cake, just let me hold you. Like I did that night you first came to me. You comforted me."

"Don't call me that!! You can't call me that!! I'm not your Nattie cake!!"

"It doesn't matter what I call you!! You are mine till your last breath and ill prove it!"

He plunged at her. She screamed as she tried to keep him from taking the scissors from her hand, but she failed. Her five foot three, one hundred twenty-pound frame was never strong enough to overpower him. Anderson stood six feet three inches tall. His broad shoulders and muscular build were more than enough to get his way. Nattalie screamed as he grabbed her wrist, squeezing and twisting until the scissors fell from her hand. He grabbed her by both shoulders and threw her to the floor. Afterwards, he stood over her as she lay on the floor sobbing. "You really wanted to hurt me Nat?" He kicked the scissors☐ across the room, then bent down to pick her up. "No, No, No, oh God please let me go!!" She wanted to fight but she was more exhausted than she had ever been. Her arms felt like limp noodles and her legs just wouldn't move. He picked her up, like a child being put to bed. The pungent smell of Liquor oozed from his breath and his body, suffocating her. It was the same nauseating stench that she could never seem to wash off completely. She felt faint. The sound of his footsteps on the hardwood was sure to haunt her dreams.

Gently, he laid her on the bed. "Don't move my love. He whispered in her ear. She moaned in pain as he roughly kissed her bleeding lips. She wanted to run but what for? She thought, "I'm ruined anyway. I'm nothing." Anderson stood over her taking his clothes off and tossing them to the floor. The sound of his belt clearing the loops of his pants sent shivers now her spine. Just as she began to mentally brace herself for the brutal intercourse that was sure to follow, Nattalie turned her head to the Landscape painting on the wall. Her mind drifted away into the image of the majestic mountains reflected in the mirror of the still lake waters. She thought of how liberating it must feel to be in that scene. She let her mind escape into fantasy as she let her cousin defile her once again.

"Nattalie. Nattalie! Hello!"

"Josh. I... I'm sorry. I zoned out there for a minute." She got up to pour a cup of coffee.

"Oh yea? You looked more than zoned out. You looked like you were nowhere on planet earth."

She sighed deeply. "I'm having second thoughts Josh. I don't think I'm the right one to be speaking here tonight."

"What are you talking about? This is your third book lecture. You were asked to be here for a reason."

"That's just it! I don't know why I'm ever asked. I didn't get a degree the same way these other speakers did. I'm not some brilliant scholar like the rest of these guys. I'm…I'm just a girl who God had mercy on. I can't even stop myself from being overcome with memories of the past."

Josh put his arm around her shoulders as she nervously held her coffee. "I know what's wrong with you. This book wasn't about theology or church history. It was about you and it's hard to bare your soul before people." Josh looked her in her face. "What you are Nattalie, is a brave woman." She shook her head and nudged him away. "No, I'm not Josh." He pulled her close again. "Yes, you are. You hear that? The conference is starting." There was a knock at the door and a woman peaked her head inside. "Ms. Blythe, you're going up first. Dr. Lawrence will be introducing you. "It's Mrs. McCurry now and thank you." Nattalie put her coffee down and said a prayer under her breath. She picked up her notebook and walked toward the door. "Hey Nattalie." She paused to look back. "Yea Josh." He walked to her and kissed her forehead. "You were made for this." She gave him a smile with tears in her eyes, then walked to the stage area.

She listened to Dr. Lawrence introduction of her from the left of the stage. For a moment she wondered who he was talking about. Words like, brilliant, talented, and passionate. Were all being applied to her and all she could feel was grateful. "So, it is my pleasure to introduce one of the brightest young Christian Apologist I've met. Ms. Nattalie Blythe-McCurry." The crowd applauded as Nattalie walked onto the stage. It was the largest crowd she'd spoken in front of since she started booking speaking engagements. Her schedule had mostly consisted of Christian clubs in High Schools and special church functions. This was an auditorium of three thousand seats with every seat full. As she looked out on the applauding crowd she began to cry. "Please forgive me for being emotional. I am truly humbled and grateful to be given the privilege to speak to you all this evening." She looked down at her notebook and noticed a sticky note on the cover that read, *you were born for this,* with a heart and a 'J' drawn in the middle of it. She smiled and continued. "I appreciate that glowing introduction Dr. Lawrence gave me. But I was just telling my husband backstage, that I'm really just a teenage girl that God had mercy on. Because of his mercy and kindness toward me in my darkest hour, I take every opportunity to defend the faith and share my testimony." The crowd applauded. "I just referred to myself as a teenage girl. I know that sounds strange because I'm thirty-three" The audience laughed. "But I always keep that time of my life close to me. I have to. I don't ever want to forget where I was when God found me. At the very bottom of the pit. I want to start by telling you about that teenage girl. Who she was and how she became the woman on this stage tonight."

Shattered

It was Easter Sunday morning and at eight o'clock the Blythe house was fast asleep. Nathan was always the first one out of bed after his mother, Lilian. He never really meant to be, but his mom and dad's room was right next to his. The sound of his mom's alarm clock, which was set to come on to the gospel station, was too loud to ignore. Sometimes he missed the days when he and his twin sister Nattalie shared a room. She would wake him up by jumping on his bed or tickling his feet. It was enough to make him scream back then but his irritation never lasted long. Not with his Nattalie. He always thought of himself as her protector, since he was a whole ten minutes older than she was. Back then Nattalie had terrible nightmares. She would end up in Nathan's bed at least twice a week with her brown curly hair in his face as she buried her tiny head in his chest. Their mother would comfort her for a while but in the end, all she wanted was Nathan. She would whine and whine for Nathan's bed, Nathan's bed. "Come on Nattie-cake." He would say to her. As soon as her head hit his pillow she went right to sleep. To say they were close would've been an understatement. Although things had changed a lot between the ages of five and fifteen, he was still her protector and the one she went to when she was afraid.

Nathan got up and slipped on an old pair of sweatpants before heading out his bedroom door. Lilian peeked out of her door after hearing his footsteps. "Oh, good you're up. Go wake your sister please. She has to be at church a little earlier since she's in the program." Nathan nodded his head and turned towards Nattalie's room. (knock knock)

"Hey Nattie get up."

"I heard her! I don't know why she thinks I can't hear from the hallway."

"Well good then hurry up and get dressed so we don't have to hear her mouth today."

They had both grown tired of their mothers constant fussing. It seemed like any disagreement was grounds for a blowout argument. The word patience had been deleted from her vocabulary years ago. Everyone, including their father, walked on eggshells whenever she was around. Especially since lately she had grown fond of throwing nearby objects when she got mad. Nattalie just wanted the mom she remembered as a toddler. Loving, always smiling, the mom who use to make up bath time songs and help her color inside the lines. In the past five years she had become someone that none of them recognized. What was once loving was now angry. Her songs were now screams. Her bright hazel eyes were like daggers when she glared. Nattalie had eyes like hers. For Nathan, looking into his sister's eyes, filled with such gentleness, was the only thing he had left to remind him of the mom he used to know.

While everyone else was upstairs hustling to get ready, Nicolas Blythe sat at the breakfast table sipping his usual cup of coffee. He was always the last to get up and the first one to be dressed and downstairs. He liked the few moments of quiet he obtained while the family was busy in the morning. He had learned to quit expecting peaceful mornings and to simply steal whatever moment he could to relax. "Daddy!!" Nattalie shouted as she came stomping into the kitchen like an angry preschooler. "Daddy I have to give my speech today for the Easter program and look what mom made me wear." She whined as she held out the hem of a green plaid dress. "Dad this is hideous! I look like a sick frog. Why can't I wear what I want?" He looked her up and down and quickly agreed with her.

"I understand how you feel pumpkin, but I believe your mom wanted you and Nate to match today."

"Yeah that was her bright idea."

Nathan said as he walked into the kitchen and sat down to pour a bowl of cereal. Just then Nattalie noticed that Nate was wearing a tie the same hideous color as her dress. She began to shed tears.

"Isn't it bad enough that I don't have friends at church! Now I get to be the laughingstock of the youth department too."

"Come on Nattie it's not that serious. Keep your voice down before mom hears you."

Nick sat down his coffee and looked at his daughters pleading eyes. She was the spitting image of her mother. Caramel skin and tight curly brown hair. Although he knew she was fifteen, for a second, she looked about four.

"Ok pumpkin, you are old enough to pick your own clothes."

"So, I can change?"

"Let's talk to your mother."

Nathan suddenly pushed himself away from the table, wiped his mouth and headed toward the patio. Seeing how aggravated Nathan was, Nattalie suddenly had second thoughts about challenging her mother's wardrobe decision.

"Uh well dad, maybe."

"It's ok Nat, we're just going to ask." He stood up from the table and called out, "Lilian!" No sooner than he completed the last syllable of her name, Lilian came walking into the Kitchen. Nick fumbled with his tie as he nervously cleared his throat.

"Lily, Nattalie was wondering..."

"Yeah I know what she wants! I can hear everything from the laundry room you know."

"Well honey the kids are old enough to pick their own clothes. They're fifteen for God's sake! It wouldn't hurt to let Nattalie wear something else." Lilian threw her hands on her curvy hips and stared at Nick like he was a child in trouble.

"Well excuse me Nick for trying to make my family look nice!"

"I'm not saying we don't look nice! I'm saying that the kids are too old to have their clothes picked out for them! Does it always have to be your way?"

"Fine! Since nothing I do is ever good enough or appreciated then wear what you want Nat!! Go naked for all I care!!"

"Oh, for heaven's sake Lilian why does everything have to be so extreme with you?"

"Why can't any of you just make me happy for once?"

The shouting continued as Nattalie slipped out of the kitchen and headed to the patio to find Nate.

The enclosed patio in the back of the house had been a sort of hideout for them since they were little. Their mom didn't like it out there because she couldn't stand the smell of their dads painting supplies, and their dad only used the patio when he was painting. So, if no one was out there, it was a safe bet that they would be alone. The high-pitched shouting from the front of the house was barely noticeable back there.

"Why couldn't you just shut up about the dress Nat?"

"Don't blame me! You agreed with me! Remember?"

"Yeah but you brought it up first. Now they're fighting, again!"

Nathan plopped down on an old wicker sofa. He was fed up with the fighting and yelling, fed up with walking on eggshells to keep from setting mom off. Even though he was aggravated with what Nattalie had done, he knew it wasn't fair that no one could simply disagree with mom without a fight. Nattalie sat down next to her twin. "I'm sorry, I just wanted to look good today. I've worked on this speech for two weeks and it's perfect. I just wanted to look perfect too. Mom had to pick out the ugliest dress she could find on the day that a hundred eyes will be on me." Nate stood up and walked to the large window that faced the back yard.

"Listen Nate! Remember last year when I wrote that poem for the black history month program?"

"Yeah why?"

"I was invisible until that day. No one ever talked to me or paid me any attention at church. It's always about you, mom, or dad. You and dad get all the attention with your wavy hair and perfect smiles. You guys look like Jet models! Mom.......well she's just beautiful. She's this big and bright personality when she's not mad. People love her." She looks at me like I disappoint her. Always criticizing my hair or my clothes or commenting on how bad my acne is getting. Nate turned from the window and sat back down next to his twin.

"You know what Nat; we look just alike."

"Only your skin is perfect, how did I end up with the muddy part of the gene pool?"

"It'll go away, I promise."

"The point is that you guys got all the attention and I got none. If it wasn't for the fact that the first lady is also my English teacher, no one would have ever known or cared that I loved to write. I don't get many moments to shine because I'm always out shined by the rest of you. I just wanted a day to feel completely good about me."

"You were never invisible to me. Look, you deserve your moment so let's just ignore the drama that's going on in the kitchen and get you out of that dress."

☐Nattalie threw her arms around her brother's neck. "Thank you. I hate when you're upset with me." Nattalie rushed back into the house to change clothes. She didn't even care that her parents were still fighting. As long as she had Nathan on her side, all was right.

It was amazing how the family could so quickly pull themselves back together. No one would've ever known that the Blythe household had been in such turmoil just an hour before they walked into the sanctuary of Life Christian Fellowship Church. After so many years of drama, they were all professional church goers. They walked in smiling, while Lilian and Nick greeted everyone with the standard "Praise the Lord" or "God bless you this morning." Nattalie was becoming annoyed with the act that her parents put on in front of the church. They barely spoke at home unless they were shouting, but the doors of the church must have been magic because they both turned into people neither Nate nor Nattalie knew as soon as they passed them. "Well good morning saints!" a voice called to them from across the fellowship hall. It was first lady December Clark, wearing her usual larger than life hat. She walked right up to Nattalie and grabbed her hand.

"I was looking for you dear. Excuse us Lilian I need her in the back so we can get everyone set for the program."

"Ok I can't wait."

"By the way Nattalie that tangerine color looks beautiful on you."

☐Nattalie smiled as she threw a quick glance at her mother's face. "Thank you, Sister Clark." They both walked off and Nattalie felt on top of the world already. Although she knew that whatever ill feelings her mother had would carry over into the evening, it was worth it just to feel like she'd won.

Later that day, the twins were relaxing at home.

"Hey Nattie." Nattalie looked up at Nate from her book on an old blanket in the backyard.

"Hey."

"That was some speech you gave today." Nattalie smiled as she looked toward the ground.

"You really think so?"

"Didn't you see the standing ovation? Didn't you see Dads face? He was about to explode with pride!"

"HA! Yea I saw him. I'm just sitting here thinking about it all. It felt really good. I wish I could feel like that all the time."

"Like what?" She uncrossed her legs, laid on her back with her hands tucked under her head.

"I wanna feel important and liked. I had the attention of that whole room and they liked me! I know you love me Nate but sometimes it feels like you're all I have."

"Mom and Dad love you Nat."

"UGHHH!!!! Mom is so unhappy all the time, I don't think she knows how to love anymore, and dad is always so busy tip toeing around mom to avoid a fight that he doesn't have time to love us!"

☐Nate laid down beside his sister but didn't bother trying to talk her out of her ideas about their mom and dad. He had often felt the same exact way. Instead he tucked his hands underneath his head and began to tell her his favorite parts of her speech that day. He raved and raved about her talent and poise as he took pleasure in his sister's smile. As long as she smiled, he would go on all day.

"Nattie!! Nathan!!" They both sat up to answer their dad. "Right here dad!" Nate called back. They both stood up and Nattalie began to gather up the blanket they had been laying on. They figured it was probably time for dinner. Daylight savings time always made them lose track of the time when they were outdoors. Dad came toward them both with the strangest look on his face. Almost like a grin but more forced.

"Ok guys, how about we go over Aunt Gene's house for dinner?"

"YES!!!!" They gave each other a high five.

"Dirty Rice, Gumbo, Crab Legs, Mmmm, Mmm." Nate said as he gazed off into the sky as if he were looking right at all the dishes he was naming.

"All right guys, we're leaving in fifteen minutes so hurry, it's almost five and you know Aunt gene likes to eat on time."

"Got it dad. We'll be ready in five minutes, its mom you'll have to light a fire under." Nattalie said with a chuckle as she ran into the house. "Mom's not coming!" Dad called out. Nattalie and Nathan both stepped back outside. "Why?" asked Nate. "As a matter of fact, where is she? We haven't seen her since we got home from church." Dad walked a little closer to them. "She said she was going to go to the park for a little walk. I guess she just needed some air or something, but since she's been so long and never told me what her dinner plans were, I figured I'd call your Aunt gene and see if she and Uncle Joe minded some dinner guest. Your mom should be home by the time we get back." The twins looked at each other and with their eyes, agreed that they were ok with the answer dad gave them.

"Aunt Geeeeene!!!!!" Nattalie squealed as she ran into the plump arms of her favorite aunt. Nate was just as excited but was playing the cool role now a days. Uncle joe must've picked up on this quickly because he walked over to Nate and greeted him with a nice firm handshake. When they were little kids, Uncle Joe would greet them with tickles and chocolate for the one who could hold their laugh the longest.

"My goodness son, you sure are getting tall. How tall are you now?"

"Five-foot eleven sir."

"Five eleven at fifteen years old? Ha! Well let's get this boy in here and feed him Gene!"

Uncle Joe stood about five foot ten and was stocky built. When Uncle Joe and Aunt Gene met back in college, he and Nick hated each other. It was mostly because Nick and Gene were so close, and he just didn't think anyone was good enough for his little sister. However, that all changed when Gene got sick. She was off work for months and on Steroids that made her gain a lot of weight. Joe never left her side. That was when he realized that he could trust Joe with his sister and as she recovered, her husband and brother became friends. "Joe move out the way so I can hug my nephew. Now I know you think you're too old for hugs and kisses, but you are still my dumpling!" Aunt Gene gave hugs so tight that Nate sometimes gasped for air afterwards. "Well come on in! I've got the Dirty rice coming out the oven now and the Gumbo is waiting on us too. Tan manje!" Nattalie pulled her dads hand. "Dad what did she say?" He whispered loudly. "Time to eat." Nick and Gene grew up speaking Creole in Louisiana. Every now and then she would slip in some words that no one but she and Nick understood.

Good times were always guaranteed at Aunt Gene and Uncle Joe's house. They laughed and ate, shared old stories, and ate some more. Nate ate so much Gumbo he was almost unresponsive. There was a peace and happiness in that house that they didn't get anywhere else. Nattalie looked up at the smiling faces of her father and brother and suddenly dreaded going home. She never saw smiles that big at home or heard laughter echoing in the halls. She thought to herself that she didn't care if her mom ever came back. If they could have happiness like this every day, she could stay gone. "Well you two look about ready to burst." Nattalie and Nate gave faint grins as they nodded their heads up and down at Aunt Gene. "Go on in the family room and put your feet up. Take your uncle with you. You know where the remote is, just don't fight over it." Nattalie and Nate nodded again and slowly staggered into the family room with a sleepy Uncle Joe right behind them. Gene looked over at Nick and took his hand.

"My niece and nephew are just beautiful and as smart as can be. Just like their Aunt Gene."

"Ha! You would take the credit for my kids Gene."

"Well who else would they get it from?"

"They do have a mother you know." Gene suddenly turned her more serious tone on.

"Yes, about their mother. Now, where is she?"

"She took a walk after church today and she hasn't made it back yet."

"Ummm, Hmmmm. How long are you going to live like this Nick? She's miserable and she's making you miserable too."

"I can't just up and leave her and my kids! I have to make it work!"
Gene sighed and leaned back into her chair. Then, she got up and without
saying a word, cut a large piece of Lemon pound cake and sat it in front of
Nick. After cutting a piece for herself, they sat and talked together a little
more. Gene hated arguments, she'd rather have cake and make memories.

On the big sectional couch in the family room was a sleeping and
snoring Nate and Uncle Joe. Nattalie wasn't quite as tired as all that. She
sat with her feet up on a velour ottoman watching her favorite show, The
Golden Girls. It was nice to watch the show without her mom commenting
on how old the characters were and how she didn't think that geriatrics
were funny. Just as she was in the middle of a good laugh, the phone rang.
First, Nattalie heard Aunt Gene's voice answer the phone in the kitchen,
then she heard her dad's voice. After a few minutes, they both walked into
the family room looking as if they had bad news. "Ummm who died?"
Nattalie said joking. "No one pumpkin. That was your mom on the phone
and she's home, so we'd better get a move on." Still he sounded as if
someone died. Nattalie wasn't ready to go. All she was doing was
watching TV, but she felt so much at peace she didn't want the day to end.
After all, who knows what's waiting at home. The last she was with her
mom; first lady December was complimenting the dress that mom didn't
want her to wear. She slowly inched herself off the cozy couch and slipped
on her shoes. She thought about just running away but the backless sandals
she was wearing wouldn't get her very far. Aunt Gene woke up Nate but
let Uncle Joe stay sleep and she tiptoed the three into the front room. She
gathered the twins up into her arms and squeezed them tight.

"Now you call your Aunt Gene. You hear? I don't care how late or
what I'm doing. If you need me, you call."

"Yes, Aunt Gene." They said in unison.

☐When she finally let them go, they both noticed the tears in her
eyes. She tended to be a bit emotional but there was something else
happening with her that neither one of them could make out. She seemed
frightened. Nick leaned in to give his sister a hug and then quickly hustled
the twins out the door.

It was a quiet car ride home. When the twins were much younger, going to Aunt Gene's house was like a mini road trip. They had to take Interstate 10 from L.A to Chino. During that hour-long trip, they would always stop for snacks and slushies at the 7ELEVEN mini mart. Nick sang along to his favorite gospel music while Nate and Nattalie played Uno in the back seat of their minivan. The ride was almost as enjoyable as being at Aunt Gene's. Nattalie sat back reclined in the front seat and thought over all the happy trips along this highway. Then she began to think about all the trips that her mom would ruin by fussing and arguing with her dad the entire way. Bills, painting the house, fixing the toilet, dishes, you name it and she could make an argument out of it. Sometimes Nattalie would ask for her dad's ear phones so she could tune out any potential arguments on the way. As she sat thinking, she realized that the minivan had been the stage for some of her most memorable moments in life up to that point, both good and bad. Mom was terrible about locking the car door, so it was her favorite hiding spot when she and Nate played hide and seek. When it was just her and her dad, it was where their best conversations took place. Once the family went camping and Nattalie met a boy named Shawn. She thought he was the cutest freckled faced boy she'd ever seen. One day on that trip, Shawn walked up to Nattalie while she was sitting in the van on the step of the sliding door. She looked up from her coloring book and saw him standing there with a bunch of flowers he had gathered. They were, yellow, pink, and purple. "These are for you." He said in a small, almost girlish voice. "I think you're pretty." She grabbed the flowers and he ran away. A smile came across her face at the thought. Some girls have to wait for their first date or prom to get flowers, but she got hers at age nine. No sooner than she completed that thought, she began to think of all the fights in that van between her parents. Mom even pulled over once to whoop Nate and ended up punching him in the lip. The blood stain was still on the seat.

Pulling up in the driveway, all Nattalie could do was think of how she could quickly get in the house and into her room without having to come in contact with her mom. The van stopped. Nick sighed and got out of the car with his twins following close behind him. As soon as the door opened, they bolted to their rooms and shut the doors. Mom was obviously waiting because no sooner than the doors shut, they could both hear her and their dad arguing. Nattalie quickly began to straighten up her room and put away anything that was out of place. If mom decided to spread her anger to her or Nate, which she often did, she wasn't going to give her one more thing to go off about.

"Where were you today?!"

"Why do you care? You and the kids just abandoned me! You could've waited for me to come home!"

"I wasn't about to spend Easter Sunday sitting here waiting for you to decide to spend time with your family! You get to disappear without telling anyone where you are, and I'm supposed to feel guilty for refusing to spend the evening waiting on you?"

"You don't love me!!"

Lilian began to cry and sob. Her tears left thick tracks in the foundation on her cheeks. She turned and started towards their bedroom.

"I deserve better than this Nick! I deserve t to be loved and spoiled. I deserve to be treated like the queen that I am!"

"What is with you woman?! It's not always about you! Loved and spoiled? When was the last time you showed me love? In fact, when was the last time you touched me Lilian? I try to get close to you at night and you turn me away. I can't even give you a kiss goodbye in the morning! Do I disgust you that bad?" Lilian sat on their bed with her eyes facing the floor.

"Look at me Lily. Can you even look your husband in the face anymore?"

As she sat there stuck for words, Nick noticed something he hadn't noticed before. Lilian was missing an earring in her left ear. If it had been any other pair of earrings he wouldn't have noticed or cared but she wore the diamond studs he purchased on their thirteenth anniversary. "Where is your earring?" Lilian raised her head and quickly reached her hands up to feel her lobes. Nick felt faint at what he saw next. "I don't know, maybe it fell out in the car." Nick's blood began to boil. Lilian stood up as if to head out to look for the earring, but he stopped her.

"Did you drop your wedding ring in the car too?" Her caramel complexion was almost white at his words.

"N….Nick I must've left it in the bathroom this morning."

"You had it on at church this morning woman!!! Don't play me like I'm some fool!!!!"

"Nick, please!" Lilian pleaded as he plunged at her and grabbed her by her throat and began choking her on the bed.

"Where were you today? All the s#!@ I've taken from you all these years and you're gonna cheat on me!"

☐Nick had lost control. She kicked and tried to fight him off, but she couldn't match his strength. Just as she was fighting her hardest, Nate came in the room.

"Dad!! Dad!! Stop!" Nate ran to pry his father from his mother's neck. He tried with all his might to pull him off of her but could not make him budge. Finally, just as Lilian felt herself losing consciousness, Nick let go. He and Nate fell back onto the floor. Lilian rolled over on the bed, gasping for air and sobbing. Nate went to his mother, still struggling to make sense of what just happened. "Mom it's okay, it's okay." She laid in her son's arms and cried like he'd never seen her cry before. His dad was sitting in the corner of the room, sobbing with his head between his legs. Nattalie, having heard Nate's voice shouting, came peaking her head into the room. She saw Nate holding their crying mother, then she saw her dad in the most pitiful state she had ever seen him. "Daddy!!!" She ran over to him and threw her arms around his neck. He looked up at his daughter and in her eyes saw her mother. Then he began to weep. He grabbed her and rocked her in his arms and comforted her. Just the way he had wanted to comfort his wife. They might as well have been shattered glass on the floor. It didn't seem like anything could put this mess back together again.

Losing Mom

Five days had passed since that drama filled Easter night. Nick left the house that night and hadn't returned. Nattalie didn't know what to think. It wasn't like her dad to just disappear like that. It also wasn't like her dad to attack her mother either. In fact, after she thought about it, she had never seen her dad cry before. Although Nate wanted to protect his mother. He knew that only something extreme could've driven his father to do what he did. Lillian hadn't said a word in explanation to the kids about what happened, and Nate was fed up with the silence.

"Mom," Nate called as he knocked on her bedroom door. "What is it?" He slowly opened the door and stepped inside. Lillian looked at her son's reflection in her vanity mirror as she continued to put on her makeup. Nate noticed the empty ring finger that had once held her custom made diamond wedding ring.

"Mom, is dad coming home?"

"Not unless he wants to be arrested. Why would you want him back anyway? You saw what he did to me."

"But what did you do to him?"

Lillian rose up from her vanity chair and walked to Nate with her finger pointed in his face.

"Now you listen here son. It doesn't matter what I did! I'm a woman and he had no right to put his hands on me!"

"I'm not saying that what he did was right mom! I've lived in this house my whole life with the two of you and never once have I seen my father out of control that way! All I'm saying is that it had to be something terrible to set him off like that."

"What about me?!! You're so concerned about what made him go off, but I'm the one covering up bruises on my neck with makeup!"

She lifted her neck to show her son the healing bruises on her neck. Nate looked away. He still couldn't believe his father could do that, but he also knew in his heart that something was terribly wrong.

"I love you mom, but I love dad too. I just want to know what's happening to our family."

"Hmmph. Today a divorce lawyer is happening. If you want your dad so bad you can go live with him at your Aunt Gene's. I'm getting my life back regardless."

Nate walked out of his mother's bedroom, hurt and disgusted at her disregard for his concern. He also wondered how he never thought to call Aunt Gene. Of course, that's where he went! Now he had to figure out how to get all the way to Chino. Dad would tell him the truth. He and Nattalie were still on spring break and as soon as Lillian left the house, he called Aunt Gene.

Nattalie was more confused than she had ever been. She frantically began packing her clothes into her pink suitcase as her brother instructed her to. "Where are we going Nate? What's happening?" Nate was busy grabbing their toiletries out of the bathroom. Nattalie began to get frightened. "Nate answer me!!" He came into her room with a plastic bag that he shoved into her suitcase.

"We are going to Aunt Genes. She and Dad will be here in less than an hour."

"Dad?? He's coming to get us?"

"I called Aunt Gene and she and Dad told me what's really been going on. We are not staying here!"

☐Nattalie wanted to ask him what he meant but she could see that he was in no frame of mind to do any explaining. So, she just kept packing. As they walked out the front door to meet Aunt Gene and their Dad in the driveway, they both noticed that the family picture that use to hang in the foyer was no longer there.

It was all like a bad dream that she couldn't wake up from. A nightmare that wouldn't end. In just one week her family was torn apart and her life turned upside down. Even though things were never perfect at least she knew what to expect out of every day. Mom's rants, followed by an argument between her and dad followed by her and Nate seeking refuge and peace on the patio. It wasn't an ideal situation, but she knew it well and she knew how to deal with it. Nattalie had no idea what to expect anymore. Nate was the only thing in her life that had not changed. She looked at her brother riding in the passenger seat next to their dad as she lay slumped over on Aunt Gene's shoulder in the back seat. Even though his face was full of worry and anger, he still looked like something out of a teen magazine. He was her north star, her constant guide. There had never been a day that she couldn't count on her twin. At that moment she decided that she was ok as long as Nate was there.

Nearly an hour had gone by since the twins arrived at Aunt Gene's. They sat in the tiny guest bedroom wondering when someone was going to tell them what was happening to their family. Nattalie laid her ear to the floor, hoping to catch a few words from the conversation that her dad and Aunt Gene were having downstairs. All she could hear were muffled groans through the floor.

"Can you hear anything Nat?" Nate whispered loudly.

"Nope. I can't make anything out. I think they stopped talking." Just then, Nate heard footsteps in the hallway.

"Nattie, quick get up!"

"Huh?" Nattalie jumped up as her dad entered the room.

"Still using your little sister to spy for you Nate? You know she was never any good at it."

"I'm not his little sister dad."

"Yes, you are, by ten whole minutes." Nate said teasing her as he reached to pinch one of her cheeks.

"Quit it!"

"Dad are you going to talk to us now?"

"Yes pumpkin, right now."

"Let's all go down to the family room", said Aunt Gene.

"I made some fresh Lemonade yesterday. How about I pour us a glass?"

The twins had been drinking their aunt's lemonade during every crisis they could remember. From broken toys to skinned knees. Rainy days when they couldn't play and the tragic loss of cherished goldfish. A glass of lemonade always seemed to make its way into the picture. The four sat down in the formal living room setting, slowly sipping their ceremonial glass of lemonade. As Nick turned toward his twins, they both sat up straight with their eyes wide, anxiously awaiting the next words from his mouth.

"First of all, I love you both with all that's in me and nothing will ever change that. With that being said, your mother and I are getting a divorce."

"That much I already know dad. Mom had no problem making that clear. I want to know why she's being so cold! It's like she doesn't care about our feelings or concern at all! Did you know that she's been out till almost dawn every night since you left? It's obvious she's checked out on this family. I just want to know why. What did we do? What did you do? What happens to us because now she doesn't want to be our mother anymore!"

Nate, who was now standing over his father, began to cry. Aunt Gene reached up to grab the glass of lemonade that was still in his hand. Nick had not seen his son so upset since he was a toddler. Just like when they were small if one was upset the other shared in the pain. Nattalie sat clutching his hand with tears rolling down her face.

"Is that all daddy?" Nattalie asked him sobbing.

"No pumpkin." He stood and placed his hand on Nate's shoulder. "Son please sit down; I'm going to tell you everything."

Nate wiped his face and sat back down next to Nattalie.

"Your mother has a boyfriend and she's moving away."

"What?" Nattalie sat up in disbelief. "Who is he? How long has this been going on?"

"A long time pumpkin. Please let me finish. His name is Roger Reynolds. I only tell you this because she intends on marrying him after she divorces me. He's an old boyfriend of hers from high school."

"Wait, didn't you guys meet in high school?" Nate asked.

"Yes, but she dated him before me. In fact, she was pregnant by him twice before I met her."

"Where are the babies then?"

"One died at birth and the other was given up for adoption. In fact, her mother sent her away to a girl's home during the second pregnancy. She never even got to hold either baby. It tore her up inside."

"So where did this Roger guy go? He just left mom?"

"No Nate, your grandmother forbad him anywhere near her after she got home. He was two grades ahead of her so when I met her my senior year he was long gone." Nick lowered his head and sighed. "She was still in love with him when I met her, but I loved her so much that I thought I could love her past her pain. I thought I could…" He choked down his tears and briefly stared up at the ceiling. "I thought I could fill the void that those babies left in her heart. When you two came along it was as if God had restored all she had lost, and we were so happy. At least I thought we were. She was the best little mother I had ever seen. She fussed over you guys constantly."

Nick stood staring out into the yard as if his eyes where focused on something. A pleasant grin came to his mouth. Then he closed his eyes as if to wipe away the image of whatever he was looking at from his vision. Remembering the wife he loved so vividly was almost too much to bear.

"She never got over losing those babies or him. When she came back from her ten-year class reunion, she was different. She saw him that night and although she said she didn't feel anything, I knew better. She's been seeing him ever since."

Nate and Nattalie both looked at each other as if a light just came on in their heads. It all made sense.

"We were seven when she went away to that reunion. That's about the time she quit singing." Nate looked over at his sister who seemed to be sharing the same memory. Their mother seemed to make up songs almost daily when they were young. Songs about breakfast, playtime, goldfish, bacon, eggs, and bath time. Anything could become a song. One day Nate was in the bath and singing one of the bath time songs she made up. She suddenly flung open the bathroom door and yelled for him to stop with that annoying noise. Nate was so startled and upset he began to cry. She never even comforted him. He never forgot it.

"So, what now?" Nattalie scowled at the thought of her mother being with another man. How she could even think of moving away was too heavy of a concept for her to wrap her mind around. "Does she plan on moving in with him wherever she's going? I guess they'll just pick up where they left off and start a new family!" She jumped up from the couch and began to cry as she ran toward the front door. Nate ran after her.

"Nattie wait! Please!" Nate grabbed the back of her blouse before she could reach the door and pulled her back into his embrace. Nattalie sobbed and could hardly catch her breath. He felt his arm wet with her tears. All her brother could think was that he wanted the simple days back. The days when all it took was her "Nattie Cake" song to calm her down. So, he did all he knew to do. He turned her around to face him. He swept her brown curls away from her hazel eyes. As he wiped the tears from her face, he started to sing her song. Nattalie, who at first wasn't amused, began to giggle. Then his voice got louder and louder as he picked her up and swung her around the room. Being that she wasn't as light as she was at age five, Nate lost his footing and they both came crashing to the floor. Only he could turn the most terrible news of her young life into hysterical laughter.

"So, what now daddy?" Nattalie asked her father who was by this time leaning against the wall smirking at them.

☐ "Where do we go?"

"Wherever you want to go pumpkin. It's your choice. I'd much rather you stay here with me, but I want it to be your choice." The twins, still sitting on the floor, looked at each other without saying a word. They didn't know where their mom was moving to or if they were even wanted there. Still with no words passing between them, only a small nod of Nathans head at Nattalie, they decided to stay with the only parent they knew would never abandon them.

Anderson

Winters were brutal in Minnesota. After almost a year of living there, Lilian still couldn't get used to it. She rushes through the airport with her suitcase rolling behind her. She hated to be the last one to show up for work. Finally, she arrives at the jet bridge and lets out a sigh of relief when she saw she was one of the first flight attendants to arrive.

"Good morning Lily." A pretty Korean flight attendant called out to her from the galley.

"Oh, hey Gwen. How was your first Amsterdam flight? I heard you had a great crew."

"Well I sobered up just in time to work the flight back home if that tells you anything."

"Sounds like my first Amsterdam trip. There's always some senior stew that feels it's their duty to break the new one in. Glad you made it back safe."

"It was great. Oh! Isn't this the week?"

"What week?"

"The week your kids come to visit."

"Oh, yea, yea. They come Sunday night."

"So, are you taking some time off?"

Lilian continued her preparation for the service in the galley. She hadn't seen her kids in nine months since she got the new job and relocated. In that time, nothing had gone as she planned for it to go. She and Roger weren't even together anymore. As badly as she wanted to see them. She was ashamed to face them.

"I can't take time off yet, but they'll be here for two weeks before school starts. My Brother and his wife are going to look after them on the days I'm working." Gwen gently patted Lilian's shoulder.

"Well that's too bad but at least you get some time with them, right?"

☐ That wasn't enough. She wanted more than just some time. She wanted to turn back time. Get back everything she had lost. Her first love, the babies she never knew. The happiness she deserved. Finding a way to have it all had become her new mission. Having some time with her kids was great but just not enough.

Flight number 2116 to Minneapolis St. Paul International Airport had just landed at 3:20 pm. Nate and Nattalie remained in their seats while the other passengers stood in the aisle anxiously waiting to exit the plane. Nate didn't like crowds and preferred not to be pushed and shoved in such a small space. Nattalie wasn't too sure about how she felt about seeing her mother after nine months. Waiting a little while longer to see her face was just fine with her.

Finally, the plane was almost clear, and it was time for the two of them to exit. They were literally almost the last ones off with the exception of a bow legged little old lady who was moving rather slowly. Instead of going around her on the jet bridge, Nate offered to assist her with her small carryon bag until they reached the airport. Nattalie knew he was stalling. Her stomach was in knots and she was sure that her twin was sharing the same uneasiness. Once they reached the airport, Nate turned to the old lady and handed her back her bag. "Thank you so much young man. I just don't get around as fast as I used to. I see my family now. They can take it from here." She pointed to a middle-aged woman and two younger boys. "My daughter and grandsons." The lady explained. Nate waved at them and watched as she walked her little bowlegs over to her daughter and fell into her embrace. He couldn't help but think that the old lady had been a good mother. That she raised her family the best she could and never left. Now she was rewarded with the pleasure of being invited to spend time with her daughter and grandsons. Maybe that was her story, maybe not. He just knew that he couldn't see that future for him, his sister, and their mother.

"Nathan." Lilian had been standing almost right behind him the whole time. He turned to see his mother standing in front of him with a nervous grin on her face. Looking just as beautiful as she always had. "Hi mom. I didn't see you." Nate reached his hand behind him to grab for Nattalie who had been silent trying to steady her nerves. "I guess you didn't see me. My son was too busy being noble." She said to Nattalie with a giggle. "Nattalie aren't you going to speak to your mother?" She walked over to her and gave her daughter a hug. "Hi mom." Her voice was almost trembling. "Can I get a hug from you too Nate?" He turned and put his arm around her shoulder. Almost the way he would hug an uncle or even their dad. Really friendly but not too affectionate. "Well I'm so happy you guys made it here safe. I have a bunch of stuff planned for us to do when I get back." Nattalie stopped, as they had been walking toward the baggage claim. "When you get back?" Lilian turned around. "Well yes sweetie. I have to work a flight day after tomorrow. It's just an overnight Florida trip. We still have tonight and tomorrow to spend together." They continued walking toward the baggage claim. Nattalie went from being nervous to frustrated. They hadn't seen her in nine months, now they only get to spend a crappy day and a half with her before she leaves again?

The car ride from the airport would have been quiet, except Lilian never could quit talking. Even if no one was listening or responding. She went on and on about the trips she had recently been on. The people she had met and wanted them to meet. She seemed to have one thousand details to give them on her life but never once asked them about how they were feeling. How they had been. As if everything was normal and nothing ever was wrong. Nate grabbed Nattalie's hand and squeezed. They knew this was going to be a long two weeks.

Emotionally and physically exhausted, they finally pull into Lilian's apartment complex. It was a pretty nice place. Walking into the living room immediately reminded them both of the home they grew up in. It smelled just like Lilian's 'Beverly Hills' Perfume. She had been wearing it for so many years that anywhere she stayed took on the scent. "What do you think guys? Like it?" They looked around the room and although Nattalie had wanted to say something nice, Nate couldn't play the game anymore.

"Listen mom. It's great that you like your job and your friends. Yea this looks like a comfortable place you have here too, but when are you going to quit acting like nothing happened?" Lilian was silent for the first time in 2 hours. "You left us mom! You left us and didn't even have the courage to tell us why you were leaving yourself. You let dad and Aunt Gene do it for you. Now you've got your new life and new job and you want to pretend that everything is ok? Well it's not!" She looked as if she wanted to cry but then she seemed to shake off the feeling of remorse.

"What do you want me to do? Huh? I'm trying to rebuild my life and make you two a part of it."

"It doesn't work that way mom. We got off that plane and you never once asked how we were doing. In fact, you haven't shown any interest in what Nattalie and I have been going through since you left. We get five-minute phone calls and post cards from whatever country you're in and that's it."

"Damn it, Nate! This is hard for me, too! I've lost everything!"

"No, you gave up everything to chase some high school fantasy! And I can forgive you but first I have to know why was that man and what you use to have more important than what you had in front of you? Your family."

Nate stood before his mother waiting for some words of comfort to come out of her mouth. Waiting for anything that might make it all make sense. Nattalie was in tears, still holding onto the polka dot book bag she had been carrying. She wanted to know too. Why her mother left. Lilian couldn't stand the look on her children's faces. They were now sixteen and she couldn't smooth it all over with kind words and a bowl of ice cream. She also couldn't face what she had done either. "I have a date tonight." She began to walk toward her bedroom. "Wait, what?" Nattalie was furious.

"I thought you were spending tonight and tomorrow with us?"

"I won't be long. Now if you want things to be normal again then I need a husband." She walked to her bedroom door and stopped.

"I'm glad you're here and I love you both. I'll fix it." Then she shuts the door. Lilian shouted from the bedroom.

"Oh, and tomorrow you'll see your uncle Charles and your cousin Anderson!"

It was painfully obvious to them both that they would never get the answers they were looking for. All they could hope for was that this vacation went by fast.

After enduring a night of the most uncomfortable sleep they could remember, the twins were dressed and waiting on their mother to drive them to Uncle Charles' house. Nattalie wasn't sure she could take a whole two weeks of sleeping on a sofa bed with Nate. He was almost six feet tall by this point. She wondered how old their mother thought they were and how it made any since for two adult sized people to sleep in that cramped sofa bed. Nate had been quiet all morning, so Nattalie decided to leave him to his thoughts rather than start complaining about the sleeping arrangements.

Finally, Lilian came from her room. "Good morning you two." She wore a bright red sweater with a sequined snowman on the front. Earrings shaped like gift boxes and boots with so much fur Nattalie wanted to ask what bear she killed to get them. "Listen you guys are gonna need some warmer coats while you're here. So, your cousin Anderson is gonna take you to the mall today and show you the sights." She boasted a huge smile as if she had just told them the most spectacular news ever. "You're ditching us again? We haven't been here for a full twenty-four hours and you're ditching us again?" Nattalie was coming to the end of her rope with her mother. Nate didn't say a word. He just sat looking out the window as if he didn't hear or care about what she just said.

"Why can't you take us to the mall, Mom?"

"Well I thought you guys would rather spend the day with your cousin than hanging with me and Eric." Now Nate couldn't stay silent anymore.

"Of course, Mom! We flew thousands of miles away from home to hang in a mall with our cousin because once again our mother finds her new boyfriend to be more important than her children! You can't sacrifice two weeks? Two damn weeks for us!"

"Don't you dare take that language with me! I still have to work while you're here, so your Uncle is gonna help me look after you guys."

"That's more of a reason for you to spend as much time as you can with us Mom." Nate stood staring at his mother. Looking for any sign that she understood how much they needed her.

"Well I'm sorry this isn't the trip you thought it would be, but I just don't have vacation time built up to take a whole two weeks off. I know you don't get it but after you guys are gone, I'm alone. I can't blow Eric off now that we're getting so close and I need someone special in my life. Don't I deserve that guys?"

☐ It was unbelievable to them both. How could she not get it? Nate wasn't interested in wasting another breath on trying to make her see what she had no interest in seeing. "Okay, well I'm not staying here. I'm calling dad and I'm going home as soon as he can get me a flight out of here." Lilian grabbed her coat and purse and stormed toward the door. "Fine! Meet me at the car, you're still going to your Uncle's." Nattalie began to pull her brother into the hallway as the door slammed. "Come on don't leave yet. Just stay with me. We can make it fun." Nate really didn't want to upset his sister, but he needed to leave. "Nattie, I'll go to visit Uncle Charles and Anderson today but I'm not staying two weeks with her." His eyes began to swell with tears. "I just got slapped in the face with the fact that I don't have a mom anymore and it hurts. Doesn't it hurt you? When did we drop to the bottom of her priority list?" Nattalie was hurt but she wanted to try to make the best of it. She was never the one to give up so quickly.

Still feeling the sting of the morning drama, the three pulled up to Uncle Charles' house. It was a very wealthy neighborhood. The houses were more like mini-mansions than regular houses. Although every lawn was covered in snow, they could tell that each one was freshly manicured in the spring and summer.

"What does Unc do for a living again?"

"He's a podiatrist." Nate raised both eyebrows and then snickered.

"A foot doctor? You'd have to give me two of these houses before I'd go near some stranger's feet." Nattalie snickered with him.

"Well he owns this home and a summer home on Lake Erie. This is Marigold Field by the way."

They could see the front door open from the driveway and what looked like Uncle Charles peeking outside. Lilian stopped them before they got out the car. "Listen, when you see your Aunt Chasity don't be surprised if she isn't looking so much like herself. She's been very ill the past few years." The twins nodded but had truthfully forgotten about her. In fact, when they started to think about it, no one really talks about her in the family. The last thing they remembered of her was a family reunion they spent in Tennessee when they were about five. Back then they called her Aunt Chassy. She had a tattoo of a heart on her left wrist and the fact that it didn't wash off was the coolest thing ever to them.

They headed toward two large double doors where Uncle Charles was standing. "Well my goodness. These can't be the twins. You were just tiny mites last I saw of you." He hugged them both one at a time, then leaned back to take a better look at them. "Charles get us inside it's freezing out here." Lilian demanded as she rushed past them into the warm house. The three quickly followed into the large foyer. It was like something out of a magazine. They didn't mean to stare with mouths gaped open, but they did. "Well kids, make yourselves at home. There is no place off limits to you. If you're hungry the kitchen is yours. If you're tired, I'll show you where the bedrooms are, and you pick which one you like best." Nattalie raised her hand slightly to interrupt.

"How many rooms are there?"

"Only six."

He answered as if to be modest. Just as Nattalie was about to ask about the number of bathrooms, a frail willowy woman came from around the corner. Although she looked nothing like they remembered, the twins immediately recognized the heart tattoo on her wrist. "Aunt Chassy?" Nate was almost in a state of shock at how a grown woman could have grown so small. He was sure he could wrap his whole hand around her waist without even trying. He rushed over to hug her in hopes that she wouldn't notice just how shocked and disturbed he was by her appearance. Her arms were so small he barely felt them around him. "My goodness you've gotten so tall and handsome." Her jittering hand touched his face and he could've teared up at any moment. He'd never seen anyone look more pitiful in his life. Nattalie walked over to give her a hug but was careful to keep a straight face. "I never thought I'd see you two again outside a family reunion or funeral." Aunt Chassy laughed to herself but even her laugh seemed labored. "Well I think I'll lay down for a while. All I need is a little water first." She was headed toward the kitchen when Uncle Charles rushed over to stop her. He gently grabbed her tiny arm and started leading her toward the staircase. "Now you know I'll bring it to you, just go on up and I'll see you in a few minutes." She looked pretty aggravated with him but walked upstairs just like he told her to. We all stood and watched her tiny legs walk up the stairs until she was out of sight. Uncle Charles started rubbing his bald head as if he was trying to remember something. "OH! I hear that you're quite a writer Nattalie. I can only assume that you like to read as well." Nattalie was still trying to process what she had just witnessed with Aunt Chassy and all she could manage to do was nod her head at his comment. "Well, let me show you my little library." Nate wanted to explore the rest of the house and their mother had made herself at home by making good use of the house phone in the family room.

He led her a short walk passed the foyer to a door. It looked like it could've been a small coat closet behind that door until he opened it. Nattalie gasped walking into the room. She had never seen so many books in her life outside a public library. She walked along the large shelves, running her fingers across the large medical manuals and textbooks. The smell of books was always pleasurable for her. "I have plenty of pleasure reading over on this side." He said pointing to the shelf across from where she stood. She rushed over to find some of her favorite authors waiting for her. By this time, he had unlocked a small liquor cabinet and was pouring himself a glass of scotch. "Nattalie you can come here as much as you like while you are in this house. I know it's been rough on you and your brother. When you need a moment to yourself, this room is yours." Just as she felt she might cry the door flung open. In walked a tall handsome boy with a mocha complexion whose eyes immediately locked with hers. "Oh, there you are son. Nattalie, do you recognize your cousin Anderson?" Nattalie barely recognized him at all. Much had changed between the ages of five and sixteen. "I would never have known who he was if you hadn't said so." Anderson laughed. "Well I could say the same. Last time I saw you, Nate was chasing you with a dead bird." They all bursted with laughter. "I can't believe you remember that." Nattalie still trying to catch her breath suddenly realized that Nate wasn't in the room. "Oh, I almost forgot we left Nate and Mom out there." Nattalie started toward the door. "I think your mom is on the phone in the family room. I ran into Nate wondering around upstairs though." Uncle Charles finished the last sip of his scotch then locked the small liquor cabinet. Anderson shook his head at his dad. "I don't know why you bother. If she wants it bad enough, she'll get it." Before his dad could respond, Anderson had grabbed Nattalie by the hand and was headed upstairs to find Nate.

It wasn't hard for Nattalie to pick which room would be hers. The walls were a bubble gum pink and everywhere was lace and ruffles. From the comforter to the curtains. It was super outdated and reminded her of something from the Victorian era. It was exactly where she wanted to be if she had to stay here for the next two weeks. Nate hadn't been very talkative since the drama that morning at their mom's apartment. He had found a room too but the only thing he cared about was the next plane out of Minnesota. Nattalie hated seeing her twin this upset. He had locked himself in the last room at the end of the hall and she wasn't going to let him spend the day by himself. Just as she began to head toward his room, Anderson came up behind her and grabbed her by her arm.

"Don't you think you should let him be for now?" Nattalie jerked her arm out of his grasp.

"I mean if he wants to go then let him go."

"What do you know about it anyway?"

"He and I talked for a minute before I came downstairs to the library. Sounds like your mom is a piece of work."

"Doesn't seem like yours is any better."

"Yea? And what do you know about it?"

"I don't know anything about it except mom said she's been sick but that's probably a lie."

"It's not a lie!! She is sick!"

The look on his face sent a chill down her spine. She had become defensive at his comment about her mom, but he had become furious at hers.

"Look, if you wanna try to force your brother to stay here when he doesn't want to then go ahead but you're not doing him any good. If I were you, I'd let him go home and enjoy what's left of his vacation."

☐ Anderson quickly walked away and down the stairs. Nattalie stood in the middle of the hallway staring at the door to Nates room. She wanted to knock on the door and beg him to stay. Instead she found herself leaving that spot to find Anderson.

Nattalie had no idea where Anderson went to. After walking through room after room and turning what seemed like a dozen corners, she suddenly felt a cold breeze gently blow her curls away from her face. When she looked to see where it was coming from, she found a set of French doors slightly opened, with Anderson on the other side of them.

He was wearing a dark blue, goose down feather coat. Warming his hands over a fire pit. Looking up from the fire pit he saw Nattalie shivering and staring at him. "It's too cold for you to be out here. Go back inside."

Nattalie shook her head. "No, I wah-want to say suh-sorry." Her lips could barely form her words. Anderson got up and walked past her into the house. At first, she thought he was still angry with her but then just seconds later he came back outside and handed her a white goose down coat.

"So much for taking you two to the mall to buy coats today." Nattalie giggled as he helped her put it on.

"I'm not in the mood for it anyway. Although I do need a better coat while I'm here. Who's is this?" She asked as he zipped her up.

"It's my mom's. She doesn't go out much anymore, especially when it's cold."

They both sat down in front of the fire pit. As cold as it was, the fire made it pretty comfortable. Anderson pulled a small bottle of liquor from his coat pocket and began to drink.

"You really shouldn't be drinking. Where did you get that anyway?"

"Same place my mom gets hers. Dads liquor cabinet."

"He locked that though."

"That crappy little lock couldn't keep mice out. Look, I know when I've had enough. I gotta have some way of dealing with the bull around here."

"So, your mom, Aunt Chassy… she's……. uh." She nervously tried to get the question to come out.

"An alcoholic." Anderson looked Nattalie in the eyes. "She's an Alcoholic and your eyes are hazel."

Suddenly the way he was staring at her made her even more nervous. She wanted to go back inside but didn't want him to be alone. So, she lowered her eyes and simply scooted over slightly away from him. She cleared her throat.

"So, who takes care of your mom while Uncle Charles is at work?"

"I do and your hair is beautiful."

☐Now she was officially uncomfortable. She started to get up. "I'm gonna go back inside now. I'm sure Nate and mom are wondering where I went." Anderson pulled her back down by her arm and kneeled in front of her. "Don't be so quick to leave cousin. This whole family is crazy, and no one is ever around for me to talk to!" He was squeezing her arms and she wanted to get up and run but the desperation in his eyes compelled her to stay right there. "I know we haven't seen each other in years but I need someone to be here for me. Just for a little while please cuz?" His eyes welled up with tears and she felt so very sorry for him. "Okay, I'll be here for you." Anderson buried his face into her chest and sobbed. Everyone needs someone, she thought. What harm could come from being there for family?

The next morning Nattalie woke up to a sun filled window. She couldn't help but grin when she opened her eyes to all that lace and pink. Just as she was about to roll over, she realized that she hadn't seen Nate since he locked himself in that room the night before. She didn't even know if he was still in the house. She threw back the pink satin comforter and headed toward the room at the end of the hall.

(knock, knock, knock) She tapped on the door. "Nate! It's me… (knock, knock, knock) Nate!" Nate opened the door so fast it startled her.

"I see you found my room. It only took you all night." He said with sarcasm oozing from his tone.

"I'm sorry…. I was about to come check on you, but Anderson said it was a good idea to let you be." Nate wiped his eyes as he sat on the edge of a huge cherry wood bed. "So, you let him give you advise about your brother now? You haven't seen him in over ten years and all of a sudden he knows what we need?" Nattalie felt terrible. She wondered, why did she let him talk her out of going to Nates room?

"It was such a crazy day yesterday…. Wait…. Did mom stay last night too?"

"Nope. She left for a date around nine o'clock. Haven't seen her since."

This frustrated Nattalie so much. She knew she wouldn't be able to talk Nate into staying the whole two weeks now. Not after he felt abandoned by both his mother and his sister. "I'm really sorry. You really gonna leave?" He pointed to his suitcase sitting at the foot of the bed. It was still packed. "Yup. I talked to dad last night and I have a flight out this evening at six O'clock. Mom ran out to go on her date before I could say anything. So, since she doesn't care to spend time with us then I don't care to inform her that I'm leaving. Uncle Charles is taking me to the airport." Nattalie's eyes began to well up with tears. She started to fight them back but then she remembered how much he hated to see her cry. So, she let the tears began to stream down her face. "Oh, come on Nattie! Don't do that!"

"I can't help it…. We haven't been apart before ya know." It suddenly hit them both. They had never been apart for more than one night at a slumber party since they were born. It was always hard to watch his sister cry, but he couldn't change his mind now. Dad had already booked his flight home. "I wouldn't have called dad last night if you would have talked to me Nattie. I don't wanna leave you here with him." She looked up at him confused by his words.

"What do you mean? With whom?"

"Anderson. That's who!"

"Sshhhh. Keep your voice down. Why would you say that?" She asked as she shut the bedroom door.

"I went downstairs to tell you I had called dad and I saw you two outside on that patio."

"We were just talking. He was upset...... He just needed somebody ya know."

"Yea well the way he grabbed you while he cried....... I just don't like it. He's our cousin but......"

"But what? He has an alcoholic for a mother and he's☐ the only one here to care for her."

"See that makes no sense. All this expensive house and they can't afford to hire a nurse or something?"

"I didn't ask all of that Nate. He was upset! Then he started drinking. I was just trying to be helpful."

Nate hugged her tight and kissed the top of her head. "Just be careful. Something just isn't right."

The Promise

For the first time in their lives, Nattalie and Nathan had spent two whole weeks apart from each other. The rest of the vacation wasn't so bad for Nattalie. She quit expecting attention from her mother and she and Anderson seemed to bond to each other. It was kind of strange not having her brother there but exciting to have someone new in her life to be close to. It seemed like they were hardly ever at the house. Anderson had his own car which made escaping the family drama a lot easier. They only had one more night before Nattalie had to catch a plane back to California and he insisted on one more late-night ride. "Slow down cuz. I can't put you on that plane tomorrow hung over." Nattalie had grown fond of drinking in the short time she'd been there. She couldn't bare the brown liquor that Anderson drank. She threw up the first night they drank together. So, the next time he made her some vodka with a lot of cranberry juice. It quickly became her favorite. She had spent half her vacation parked with her cousin in an abandoned truck stop, drinking and talking. "I'm not gonna be hung over. Mom is too busy up under that new boyfriend to notice me anyway." Nattalie reclined her seat back and unzipped her coat.

"Don't be so sure. Parents have a way of ignoring you till you do something that makes them look bad." She giggled.

"Yea I guess you're right. God only knows what goes through my moms' head sometimes."

"I don't believe in God."

"Well, why not?"

"It's simple. There's no proof of any such thing. Besides, if there is a God, he's either weak or doesn't care at all. Why else would the world be so messed up?"

Nattalie didn't quite know how to process what he was saying. "The way I see it is, we all have to decide what's best for us and make our happiness wherever we can find it. 'Cus in the end, it's simply lights out." Being too intoxicated to try and understand him, she just turned up the music and continued drinking. Anderson sat staring at Nattalie who was sipping her drink and humming along with the music in the car.

"What is it?"

"Uhh… nothing I just had an idea. It's only seven and I don't feel like sitting here tonight. I don't wanna go home either." Nattalie sat up from her seat. "Soooo what's the plan?" Anderson took the car out of park and began to drive. "Where are we going?"

"To a little motel in the city. Only twenty minutes away."

"Why would we go to a motel."

"I'd rather sit back and watch TV ya know? It'll be more comfortable to hang out there than in a car. I know a place that lets you pay by the hour."

☐"Okay, but… what motel lets you pay by the hour?" Anderson started to laugh. "Don't worry about it. I know a place. We'll hang for a couple of hours then I'll get you back so you can get rest for the flight." They didn't talk much during the trip. Nattalie mostly thought about how much she missed her brother and her dad. She wasn't excited about leaving Anderson though. She felt sorry for him being a Seventeen-year-old caretaker for an alcoholic mother. When Uncle Charles got home it seemed like he raced to grab Nattalie and leave the house. Who would he escape with now?

They pulled up to what almost looked like a box office at a movie theater. The flashing red 'vacancy' sign looked as if it could fall down at any moment. Going to a motel to hang for a little while didn't seem like a bad idea at first but this place was gross looking. Anderson put the car in park and walked up to the window where the attendant looked like he hadn't bathed in weeks. They were talking, she assumed about the price of the room, when the attendant moved his head to the side to get a look at Nattalie. After a few seconds he nodded his head and gave Anderson the key. She was definitely uncomfortable now. Especially since there was another man smoking by the side of the building that was now staring and smiling at her. Anderson got back into the car and began to drive around to the room. "What were you and that guy talking about? Why was he looking at me?" He parked the car in front of motel room door. "He thought you looked underage. I told him you were eighteen." Nattalie thought for a moment. "Wait but you're not eighteen."

"No, I'm not but I have fake I.D." He got out of the car and went to open the door. "You coming or not?" Nattalie reluctantly got out of the car and followed him into the room.

The room obviously hadn't been updated since the 70's. It smelled like old cigarette smoke and beer. "Don't they clean these places after people leave?"

"Yea I'm sure they do, it's just super old décor. I don't care though. Come sit down and have a drink and relax." Relaxing was going to be a challenge in this place. She suddenly just wanted to go home. "Hey, we can't stay long. My flight leaves at noon and we have to be at the airport…" Anderson started laughing. "Chill out cuz. I'll get you back in time to pack and stuff. Here have a drink and sit down on the bed." He held out a flask he pulled from his inside coat pocket. "I don't like drinking that stuff straight. You know that."

"Just… take a few sips to relax. That's all." She rolled her eyes at him and took the flask. Taking even a small sip of the cheap whiskey was like torture to her. "YUCK!" She wanted to throw it back up. Anderson fell back on the bed laughing. "That's so not funny."

"You are such a light weight cuz. It's so cute." Nattalie sat down on the bed next to him, wiping her mouth. "Well turn on the TV or something. Isn't that why we came here?" Anderson laid back onto the pillows and turned the TV on with the remote. "You are way tense tonight cuz. Come lay back with me." She laid next to him on the bed and tried to be comfortable but the cigarette smell in the comforter was making her nauseated. She didn't want to ruin a relaxing evening for him so she asked for another drink so she could chill out a bit. She took several sips this time. "Slow down! I'm not taking you back to my house sick. Dad will kill me." She was definitely tipsy but didn't care so much about the room anymore. Anderson turned over to face her and took another sip from the flask. "I'm really going to miss you. You've been like my best friend these past couple of weeks." She had noticed that he really didn't have many friends. "Yea it's been fun. You took my mind off my mom and her drama. She spent more time with her boyfriend than me. Even though she won't get to see me again till summer." Tears started welling up in her eyes. Anderson had kept her occupied so much that she hadn't really stopped to think about how much that hurt her. "I just want my mom back I guess." He moved in to hold her and wiped the tears from her face. "You know my dad has helped out with my mom more than ever since you've been here. I guess he wanted you to have a good time. I don't care why. I just know that things are better when you're here." They both had tears running down their cheeks. Nattalie was so glad to be able to talk to someone who understood and to be able to be there for him too. "I wish you didn't have to go. Promise me we'll always be there for each other." Nattalie looked him in the eye. "I promise." With those words, Anderson kissed her on the lips. She knew that this shouldn't be happening. Her mind started racing. This was her cousin. This wasn't right. "Stop it!" She pulled away and jumped off the bed. "Take me back now!" Anderson stood up with tears running down his face. "You just promised you'd be there for me. I need you now. Just let me feel you as close to me as possible. Please don't turn away. I don't want to be alone anymore." She couldn't move. It felt like she was betraying him to walk away and she knew all too well what it felt like to be left alone. He moved in close to her and pulled her in by the waist. He began kissing her hard, but she didn't kiss back. Her thoughts were screaming for her to run but her body wouldn't respond. He began removing her clothes and she wanted to run still but couldn't make herself move. He stood naked in front of her, looking at her perfect skin and young figure. She didn't want to look at him but he lifted her head so their eyes could meet. "We belong to each other. We are blood, connected forever." Then he picked her up and laid her on the bed. She was afraid. She knew what was happening but couldn't figure out how it got this far. Her hands were crossed over her breast in an attempt to cover some part of herself. She could feel his hands running all over her shaking body. It was impossible for him to not know how scared she was, but he continued. She covered her mouth so she wouldn't cry out loud. She felt completely helpless and closed her eyes tight as he laid all his body weight on top of her and jammed himself into her repeatedly. She screamed and he covered her mouth. Between the pain and not being able to breath because of his body weight and now his hand over her mouth she felt completely powerless. She began frantically trying to push him off. Then he took both her arms and pinned them above her head. Finally, after what seemed like an hour, he let out a loud groan and stopped. The tears streamed down both sides of her face and the only thing she could feel was the pool of sweat he'd left on her chest. The rest of her body had gone numb. He raised his body from hers and smiled at her. Nattalie was more confused, in more pain and felt more betrayed than she had ever felt before.

Big Sister

"Hey dad, I told you the flight was gonna be late. You owe me five bucks." Nathan and his dad sat at the baggage claim waiting for Nattalie's flight to land. "Well son I'd rather be too early than too late." Nate laughed. "Whatever, pay up!" Nick laughed and reached in his pocket for a five-dollar bill.

"Here but I'll win it back before the day is over."

"If you say so dad."

Nick had enjoyed having his son home by himself the past couple of weeks. It seemed like their whole world had been centered around coping with his mom leaving and trying to gain some normalcy back into their lives. They had spent the entire winter break between the gym and the basketball court. Nattalie was always the one Nate opened up to, but he discovered that he had a father that was just as easy to talk to. In fact, he figured that was a trait that Nattalie got from him. Although they had both missed her so much. They were a little sad to see their time alone end. After about an hour Nattalie was finally on her way down to baggage claim. She began running her hands through her hair and tugging at her clothes as she got closer to the escalator. She felt nervous. Would they be able to tell? The soreness between her legs made it difficult to walk without pain. Panic started filling her stomach. She was convinced that they would take one look at her and know something was different. Before she could really pull herself together Nate spotted her and was yelling out her name. Suddenly she was wrapped up in her brother's embrace, He lifted her from the ground and began to swing her back and forth. The nervousness she had been feeling suddenly turned into relief. This was her brother. Her safe place. She was home and no one would hurt her again.

Five months had gone by since Nattalie had returned from winter break. Five months since she had seen her mother but only a few weeks since she'd last heard from Anderson. He made it a point to call at least once every couple of weeks since she left. Some days she could get her dad to take a message for her, but she knew if she started avoiding Anderson too much dad would start to ask questions. So, she reluctantly held small talk with him until she could figure out an excuse to get off the phone. This had been going on for five months and now she was only a few weeks away from summer vacation and another trip to Minnesota. The thought of getting back on a plane and traveling thousands of miles to be ignored by her mother and possibly violated by her cousin was enough to make her physically ill. All she could think of was how she could get out of going. Her mom hadn't made any reservations yet. Maybe she could make herself sick or at least pretend to be sick. She wasn't sure if her dad would fall for the thermometer on the light bulb trick anymore. She just knew somehow, she had to stay home.

Walking home from school with Nate, Nattalie hardly said a word. He knew something was wrong but didn't want to ask. She had seemed so guarded since she'd been home. Suddenly she was locking her bedroom door when she never used to. If anyone asked about her trip, or mom or Anderson she changed the subject. Something wasn't right and he had finally had enough of the subtle changes that had seemed to come between them. Just as they started to walk up the driveway he stopped her. "Hey Nattie, we gotta talk. What's going on with you?" Nattalie wanted to talk to her brother but was terrified of what telling him would do to her family. It was best in her mind to try and forget it and avoid it ever happening again. "Look I'm sorry. I'll be okay really." Nate wasn't at all satisfied with her response but before he could ask another question, he noticed that she was now staring at the house with a strange look on her face. "What are those in the window?" Nate looked as she pointed at the large window in front of the house. "It looks like curtains. Nice ones too. Since when does dad care about nice curtains?" They both giggled and headed inside to find out what the new purchase was all about. Lilian had always wanted to decorate the living room just like the ones she use to see in the magazines. Her dream was a fancy house to entertain guest in, but Nick was never going to spend his hard-earned money just to impress someone else. If he bought it, it was because he wanted it. "Hey dad!" Nate called out. "So, what's with the new décor?" They came into the living room to find an attractive woman in a navy-blue cardigan sitting on their couch. "Oh, you must be Nathan and Nattalie." The woman stood up to greet them. "Uhhh yea, yea, that's us and umm you are?" Nathan held out his hand to shake hers. "I'm sorry my name is Antonia, but I go by Toni. Good to finally meet you guys." Nate nodded and smiled politely. Still wondering who this woman was, he noticed that Nattalie hadn't said a word. She had been examining Toni from the moment she laid eyes on her. Her appearance was neat and classy. She wore a single strand of pearls around her neck. Her face framed hair cut laid perfectly without one hair out of place. Her makeup was flawless but not at all heavy and she smelled like vanilla. The scent fluttered in the air. Nathan nudged her in the arm to snap her out of the apparent trance she was in.

"What? ... Oh hi. I'm uhh."

"You're Nattalie." Toni could see that she was a bit bothered. "Well you're just as pretty as your pictures and that hair is gorgeous. Those curls are to die for."

"I get them from my mother."

Nattalie snapped but wasn't at all sure why she said that. She never wanted to be compared to her mother in anything. All she knew was that this woman's presence put her on the defense. "Hey you two!" They turned around to see their dad walking into to the living room. "I'm sorry I had to take a call in my office. I was hoping to properly introduce you three." He walked over to Toni and put his arm around her shoulders. "Well since you've met. I invited her over today to let you know that we're dating and have been for a little while." Nattalie felt sick but she couldn't figure out why she was so upset. "Cool. I mean dad if you're happy then we're good with it. Right Nattie?" Nattalie dropped her book bag in the middle of the floor and ran toward the backyard. Nick called out her name and started to run after her. "No dad! I'll go get her." First, he thought she would be in their old spot on the patio. Then he realized that she wanted to be alone so she was going where dad or Toni couldn't follow. When they were much smaller, they found an old rusty ladder in the garage. One day Nate used it to climb on top of the roof of the garage and talked Nattalie into coming up with him. Other than the patio, it was a favorite hiding spot for Nattalie whenever she couldn't take her mom's yelling and carrying on anymore. Nate went around the back side of the garage and saw the ladder. When he climbed up, there she was. On the back side of the roof, out of sight with her head buried in her knees. He sat next to her and pulled her close to his side.

"She seems like a nice lady Nattie." She wiped the tears from her face.

"Yea she does huh."

"Then why are you so upset? Do you want mom back home?"

"No!... I mean yea... but...I don't know."

Nattalie wasn't sure what she wanted. She couldn't stand the person her mother was. She resented her for making their lives miserable when she was still there then leaving. Still it hurt to see her dad with his arm around someone else. To know that things were truly never going to be the same again. "I'm glad he's moving on ya know? He was smiling pretty big. He never smiled like that with mom." Nattalie brushed her hair away from her wet face.

"No, I guess he didn't. None of us did."

"Hey, it's gonna be different but let's give her a chance. Okay?" Nattalie nodded her head.

"If it doesn't work out, at least we know where the new curtains came from."

☐Nattalie laughed. "Yea.. at least."

School was finally out but unlike most teenagers, Nattalie couldn't have been more upset to see the year end. She didn't want to go back to see her mother. The thought of ever coming face to face with Anderson again made her sick to her stomach. But staying home meant a whole summer with Toni. Who had made herself quite comfortable at their house over the past month. Nick never had her stay the night. Always concerned about setting a good Christian example for them. She'd stay over till dad got sleepy but was right back there the next morning. Nate was rather happy about her being around so much. She made his favorite chocolate chip pancakes for breakfast and made a fuss over his interest in math and science. They seemed to get along so well, and it made Nattalie happy to see Nate so happy, but it also made her jealous. It was like he found another mom, but she hadn't. It was starting to look like she had no place at all where she felt completely comfortable or safe. Staying home for the summer was certainly a better idea than going to see her mom but she had no idea what excuse she could come up with not to go.

"Hey Nattie Cake!" Nate came into the kitchen particularly happy, which was annoying to Nattalie who had far too much on her mind to be so happy. "What are you so happy about?" She asked barely looking up from her cereal bowl. "Why aren't you happy? It's the last day of school!" Nate tore open a box of donuts and continued talking with his mouth half full. "Look, I dunno what's been eating you, but the summer is here. I wanna have some fun with my sister like we always use to." Nattalie continued playing with her cereal. "I was even thinking that maybe we wouldn't visit mom this summer." Nattalie's head turned so fast she actually cracked her neck.

"Ouch…"

"What happened?"

"Nothing, what did you say? Are you serious?"

Nate sat down next to her. "Of course, I am. I don't wanna spend my summer the way Winter break began."

She threw her arms around her brother's neck. She just knew that once dad knew that neither one of them wanted to go back, he wouldn't make them go. "When can we tell dad?" Nate gulped down a glass of milk. "Let's catch him before he leaves for work." They both hurried upstairs to see their dad. Nate knocked on the bedroom door.

"Hey dad, you dressed?"

"Yup, come in."

They didn't go in that room much. Not since that awful day when their parents fought. So, the first thing they noticed was the brand new and expensive looking comforter on the bed, with matching curtains. "Nice comforter dad." Nattalie gave a forced grin to poorly hide her annoyance. It was no mystery where it came from.

"Well thank you sweetie. It was a gift from Toni."

"Yea I figured, but Nate and I have something to tell you."

Nick finished adjusting his tie. "Okay shoot."

"Well Nattalie and I were wondering if it was possible for us to just stay home this summer."

Nick looked puzzled for a second. "Anything going on that I should know about?"

"Nothing I didn't already tell you when I came back last time."

"I see. Well I'm okay with that but your mom wanted you guys to come. She's got some news she wants to share with you two."

"Do you know what it is?" Nattalie asked.

☐"Yes, I do but it's not my place to tell you. It's not bad news by the way." Nick grabbed his wallet and keys from the dresser. "Look I gotta run, call your mom after school. Let her tell you." He patted Nate on the back and walked downstairs.

It felt like that last bell would never ring but there it finally was, and summer had officially started. Feeling much lighter on her feet than that morning, Nattalie hurried out of school to meet Nate. Standing at their usual spot she was becoming irritated that he wasn't there yet. Just when she was about to turn back to find him, he popped up. "Where have you been?" Nate smirked and then turned to wave at a pretty cheerleader who was blowing kisses back at him. Nattalie rolled her eyes as far back in her head as she could.

"Ohhh so that's what was holding you up."

"Yea whatever sis lets go home so we can call mom and get this over with."

She had almost forgotten about the news they were supposed to get from their mom. Truthfully, she didn't care what the news was. She had a whole summer ahead of her and all she could think about was being at the pool with Nate, hanging out at the mall. Maybe even some weekend getaway trips to the lake. She'd spent the past five months dreading going back to Minnesota for the summer. Now she could relax.

"Hey Toni!" Nattalie greeted her with a smile when she practically skipped into the kitchen. "Hey Nattalie." Toni was quite surprised at her chipper demeanor, especially toward her.

"Did you have a good last day?"

"Yup!" She reached in the fridge for an apple juice. "I'm 'bout to call Kelsey and see if she wants to stay over."

"Shouldn't you ask your dad first?"

"He won't mind."

Kelsey had been a new face around the house for a few weeks. She was becoming almost as regular a visitor as Toni. □ "Well let's call mom first Nattie." Nate came into the kitchen already with the phone to his ear. It barely rang before their mom answered. "Hi mom… we're fine. I'm gonna put you on speaker okay?" He sat the phone down on the counter.

"Okay we're here."

"Hey Nattie! How was the last day of school?"

"It was good mom."

"Well I can't wait to see you guys. I have some exciting news."

"About that mom…" Nattalie interrupted. "Nate and I decided that we want to spend the summer here." The phone was silent for a brief moment.

"What do you mean?"

"We just want to stay here that's all. With our friends in our house like we spend every summer." Nate knew that this was about to be an argument, but he didn't care. "It's because of that woman isn't it? She's poisoned you against me!" Toni was still in the kitchen, drinking the sweet tea she'd made for them the day before. She didn't say a word. Just sat her glass down on the counter and quietly walked out of the kitchen. Nattalie hadn't been a fan of Toni's but in that moment, she was sorry she had to hear that.

"Mom, Toni has nothing to do with it! We just would rather be home."

"Oh, I see. I'm already by myself and now my own children won't even come see me."

It was frustrating for the both of them. Everything was about her. No matter what.

"Mom we're sorry but it's what we want to do."

"Fine then! Stay there while I spend the summer depressed and alone!"

Nattalie once again rolled her eyes as far into her head as she could get them.

"Wait what happened to that guy you were dating?"

"Ugghhh he left me. I guess nobody wants me." She began to cry and sob into the phone. Nattalie had had enough. "Listen I'm sorry about that but our mind is made up and dad says its ok." Lilian let out a few more sniffles. "Fine. Well since you're not coming, I may as well tell you now.

You have a big sister." They both looked at each other, remembering what their dad had told them about the baby she had in high school.

"Dad told me and Nate already about the babies you had in high school and the adoption."

"But I found her." Another brief moment of silence came over the room.

"So, you've talked to her?"

"Yes, yes! Her name is Valencia and she lives in Georgia now." Neither one of them knew quite what to say. Nate spoke up first.

"That's great mom. Do we get to meet her?"

"I was trying to get her to come here while you guys were in town for the summer but that's ruined now, I guess."

"Maybe not. I mean she could come here to meet us sometime."

"I want all my children together! Just the way it was supposed to be."

They really didn't know how to feel. After finally ending the conversation with their mom, Nate went to find Toni.

Nattalie couldn't make sense of anything that was happening. Why her mother couldn't just be happy knowing they were spending the summer the way they wanted to, was beyond her. Why after all this time had she decided to find her other daughter? Why the heck was Nate clinging to Toni so much lately? Nothing was making any sense. She started walking slowly through the house with her thoughts tumbling all over themselves. Meanwhile Nate and Toni sat on the patio enjoying the pretty day and pleasant conversation. Nattalie had been passing back through the kitchen when she heard them laughing. Curious about what could have been so funny, she walked out to join them. On the old whicker sofa sat the two of them with smiles bigger than that room had seen in years. He wasn't upset at all which just added another mystery to her list.

She was still quite irritated with what had just happened on the phone. Toni looked over to see her standing there with a puzzled look on her face. "Hey lady. Come sit with us." She moved a pillow out the way as Nate moved over to an even older rocking chair.

"What's that playing on the stereo?"

"It's Johann Pachelbel. He's my favorite composer. Although some consider him to be a one hit wonder. "She giggled to herself as she said it. Nattalie looked confused. She had never really paid much attention to classical music. Even though her dad used to play it often. Especially after fights with mom when he wanted to be alone. Her mom hated classical music. She was never sure if he played it to calm himself after a fight or just to irritate mom. It had been a while since she had heard it in the house. The sound of the violins brought back memories that hurt more than she'd ever dared to admit and something broke inside of her. At that moment and she began to cry. Toni sat up and put her arms around her shoulders.

"Hey sis, what's wrong? It's gonna be okay. I won't let mom ruin the summer; I promise."

"It's not that Nate. I'm just tired and want something to be normal for once. I don't wanna even have to worry about the summer or some long lost sister coming to town! I just…. I just wish we had a real mom ya know? "

☐ Toni still had her arm wrapped around Nattalie's shoulders but didn't say a word. Just held her. After a minute of trying to choke down tears, she let go of all the ill feelings she'd had toward Toni and began to sob into her shoulder. Rocking back and forth in Toni's arms was a comfort she'd been missing. Now she knew why Nate had been clinging to her so much. It was the closest he'd had to a real mom in a long time.

Unwanted Surprise

Three weeks into summer break and the days had been ideal. Hot afternoons at the pool. Bike rides on the trail with Nate. Nattalie's new friend Kelsey made shopping trips with her in between the outdoor activities. Which made Nate happy because now he wasn't forced to go to the mall with her anymore. In the month since Kelsey and her family moved into the neighborhood, she had become a part of the household. Besides Nate, no one had ever been in her space this much. Everything was perfect. It was enough fun and laughter to make her forget every sorrowful event of the past six months. Dad even woke the family up for church on Sunday morning and took everyone horseback riding afterwards. It had been so long since they had done either one. Years of playing church when their mom was there had worn him out on the very idea. However, he was seeing things with new eyes it seemed. With Toni at his side along the way.

After a long afternoon of riding the dusty trail they turned their horses around and headed back to the stables. Heading down the highway for home, Nattalie looked back from the front seat to see Toni and Nate sleeping. In that moment, she felt like she had a whole family again.

It was almost completely dark when the tired foursome came stumbling into the house. Toni sat down on the sofa and almost immediately popped back up. "Whoops! I almost forgot I've been on a horse all afternoon. I'd better get home and shower." Nick leaned in to kiss her cheek.

"Okay sweetie. See you tomorrow?"

"Of course, you will".

She blew kisses in the twins' direction. "Bye you two." They waved from the kitchen "Bye Toni!" Nattalie actually hated to see her go. She had been part of that perfect day. Her company was pleasant. She was funny and knew all about horses. She even packed sandwiches for everyone. Nattalie was almost lost in these thoughts when she noticed the red light blinking on the answering machine.

"Dad! Looks like you've got messages!"

"Check 'em for me please!" He called back from his bedroom. Nattalie hit the play button and her stomach instantly began to turn at the sound of the voice coming from the machine.

"Hey, it's mommy. Listen…. I've decided to come out there to see you guys since you don't wanna come see me. …… Anyway, I'll be there in two weeks and I'm bringing a surprise! See you then… OH! And by the way, your Aunt Chassy passed this morning so pray for your cousin and uncle. See you soon."

Nattalie suddenly felt deeply sorry for Anderson. Even though she had been trying to forget what happened. Her heart ached for him and she almost picked up the phone to call him. But she couldn't. All of her happy thoughts were suffocated all at once by one voice message. Now her brain was going a mile a minute trying to figure out what the "surprise" could possibly be. How her mother might manage to ruin her summer after all. Nate had to hear about all of this. She knocked on his bedroom door and called his name, but he didn't respond. So, she peeked inside to find him fast asleep and snoring across his bed. They were all tired, but she couldn't rest now. She needed to talk but now she could hear her dads shower running. She knew he'd be heading straight for bed afterwards. It was just her and her thoughts all night long. What a long worrisome night it was.

Having barely slept all night, Nattalie was awakened by the smell of her dad's coffee brewing. She jumped up to finally tell him about the message. Just as she was getting to the part about Aunt Chassy, Nate walked into the kitchen.

"Wait, what happened? Who died?"

"Aunt Chassy, and mom is coming in two weeks." Nate opened the fridge to grab some apple juice.

"Why?"

"I don't know. Something about coming here cuz we won't come there."

"Now wait a minute you guys." Nick pulled out a stool from the counter and began stirring cream in his coffee.

"She's still your mom. I know she can be difficult."

"And selfish and self-centered."

"Okay Nattie... okay. Look she wants to see you guys. You're still her children. Just try to make the best of it. You don't have to spend every waking moment with her." Nate sat down at the counter.

"What about Toni?"

"What do you mean?"

"You know mom doesn't like her. You know she's gonna try and press her buttons just because she's petty and childish." Nick wanted to say something, but he knew Lilian too well. He knew Nate was right.

"I'll handle that, don't worry about Toni."

"Yea Nate I'm more worried about this so-called surprise." They all sat at the counter sipping and drinking and eating without saying a word. Then Nate blurted out.

"The sister!"

"Huh?? You think so?"

"Yup. It's the most recent big news. It's gotta be."

She really didn't know what to think about the whole long-lost sister thing. It was kind of exciting but weird at the same time. What would she say to her? What would she be like? Would she be like her mom?? That was a terrible thought to her. She shook her head as if to shake away all the thoughts running through her mind. "You know what, I have two weeks until my summer is possibly ruined." She got up and headed toward her room.

"Where are you going Nattie?" ☐

"I'm getting dressed and going to get Kelsey! I gotta get all the fun I can get!"

The days didn't seem like whole days. They seemed more like brief moments that none of them could hold onto. Nattalie looked at her watch constantly. As if somehow that would pause time and prolong her happy moments. She sat in her room with Kelsey listening to Mariah Carey's latest album. Kelsey sang along while flipping through a "Seventeen" magazine. Nattalie loved Mariah and admired how Kelsey could almost hit those high notes just like her. She watched her friend as her hoop earrings swayed along with her flat ironed hair to the music. She wanted to feel that good and that free. But all she could think about was how her fun was about to end. There was never any peace when her mother was around. Only frustration, anger, and sadness. She had tried to be positive when she visited for Christmas. In the end, she was left alone and taken advantage of.

"Girl what's wrong with you?!! You've been pouting all day."

"I don't know... I guess I'm just..."

Nattalie wanted to confide in her friend what was really going on in her head, but she knew the only one that would understand was Nate.

"Is it your crazy momma? Cuz you know you can just come hide out at my house If it gets ugly." Nattalie laughed.

"Yea I know... I'm cool. I just need to get out today."

"Time for the mall??"

☐ "Time for the mall!" And off they went.

The morning was finally here. It almost seemed like a relief. She had been on pins and needles about it for two whole weeks. The uncertainty of what drama she may or may not bring. The "surprise" that was coming. It had all been too much. No matter what came next, at least all of the guessing would be done with. Nattalie lay in bed the morning of her mom's arrival and let these thoughts walk through her mind. (knock, knock, knock) "Hey you up?" Her dad peeked his head into her door. "I'm up." She sat up out of bed and sighed deeply.

"It's gonna be okay sweetheart. Just give it a chance. She's still your mom."

"I know daddy. I'll try, I promise."

She wasn't sure she really meant what she said but it didn't matter anyway. If drama was flying in that morning, then she just had to be ready for it. "I'm headed to pick everyone up from the airport. So, get dressed." Nattalie nodded as her dad left her room. Just as she started going through her drawers, she realized what he had just said. "Did he just say everyone?" She ran to find out who 'everyone' was, but he was already leaving the driveway. "What's the matter with you?" Nate saw her run to the door as their dad pulled off. "Nothing. I'm getting dressed."

Now the time slowed down almost to a halt. She tried to make it go faster by cleaning up the house. Although it was virtually spotless. Her mind kept going back to when she and Nate where little. How they clambered to clean up their room to keep mom from getting angry. A messy room was a whooping for sure. Sometimes so bad it would leave marks they would have to hide from their dad. They never told him a lot of things. After what seemed like an eternity, they finally heard the car pull up into the driveway.

The both of them came rushing out the front door onto the porch. They wanted to see who was in the car. In the front passenger seat was obviously their mom. In the back seat was a woman who's face they couldn't make out. Nate grabbed Nattalie's hand as the doors opened and everyone stepped out. A tall caramel skinned woman who looked like the missing triplet of Nattalie and their mother stepped out of the car. They stood there with mouths gaped open. No doubt she was their sister. Their hearts were full at the sight of her. What had they been so anxious about? She deserved to know her real family and they deserved to know her. Just as they both were ready to walk over to the car to help with the bags, someone else they hadn't noticed stepped out of the back of the car. Nattalie's face flushed clean of its color. She let go of Nate's hand and slowly began to take steps backward. "Nattie? Nattie what's wrong? Nattie?!" Her body locked in place as her eyes locked with Anderson who was smiling at her from the driveway.

As soon as she gained just a little feeling in her leg, she forced her body to move as quickly as she could into the house. Nate called after her, but she was gone before he could find out what was upsetting her. Just as he was about to go after her, his dad called him. "Come help with the bags son!" He walked over to the car where they were still pulling suitcases from the trunk. Nate was so concerned about Nattalie that he briefly forgot about the new sister. "Hey sweetie!" His mom aggressively wrapped her arms around his neck and began to rock him back and forth.

"Okay, okay mom let go, you're strangling me."

"Oh, quit exaggerating. Can't I be happy to see my only son?"

Just then he came in eye contact with a woman that so closely resembled Nattalie he for a split second thought she'd come back outside.

"Well where is your sister? I wanted you both to be here for this."

"She's not feeling good mom. I'll check on her in a minute though."

"Well okay. This is Valencia. This is your sister."

She stood there with her arms extended toward Valencia as if she were presenting a prize on 'The Price is Right.' "Yea. I figured that." He held his hand out to shake hers. She reached out to shake his hand, but he could tell she was quite nervous. Her hand was shaking.

"I'm Nate. I guess I'm your brother."

"Nice to meet you." She said in an almost hushed tone. "Well wait a minute. Now where did Anderson go?" Their mom looked around for him. "He took a couple of bags inside." Nick said as he closed the trunk. "That's where we all should be." Nate grabbed the bag next to Valencia and headed into the house.

Meanwhile Anderson walked through the house alone, looking for Nattalie. Although it was a ranch style home, it could easily be a maze for anyone who was unfamiliar with the layout. He called her name softly as he walked down the hallway. But no one answered. She sat in her room crouched in the corner as quiet as she could be. The sound of his voice did something to her senses. She suddenly could smell the alcohol on his breath and the stench of cigarettes on the comforter of that cheap motel. She felt ill. She wondered how long he would be here and just why on earth her mother would bring him here. Right as she was about to start crying, she heard Nate's voice in the hall.

"Did you lose something cuz?" Nate walked up behind Anderson and placed his hand on his shoulder. Nate hadn't been fond of him at all during their trip to Minnesota. So, to find him wondering his home calling for his sister without ever having said hello was concerning to him.

"Oh, hey cousin! Good to see ya, man. I was just looking for Nattalie."

"Yea I see that. She's not feeling well so uhhh…you should probably go into the living room with the rest of the family." Nate was definitely not liking this.

"Hey it's cool. You know me and Nattie got real close last winter so I just was excited to see her ya know."

"Like I said, she's not feeling good."

Anderson turned around and headed toward the living room. Little did he know that he was practically in front of her room and she heard everything. Smiling to herself she remembered that Nate wasn't there with her last winter, but he was here now. Nothing bad was going to happen with her brother there to protect her.

"Okay everybody, smile!" Lilian yelled out to her children gathered on the front lawn for a picture. Their reluctant smiles made it obvious to anyone who was looking at them, that they were quite uncomfortable with the situation. It was obvious to anyone but Lilian. She was a master at seeing what she wanted to see. In this case, she wanted a happy tear-filled reunion with her children. Where they all got along, instantly loved each other and were glad to be there with their mother. Nothing could have been further from the truth. Nathan and Nattalie were strangers to Valencia. Although she wanted to believe that she'd bonded with Valencia during the trip, Lilian was a stranger to her too. She may have been Lilian and Nattalie's triplet but she'd grown up in the country and was used to a quieter life. Just the traffic on the way from the airport was quite overwhelming for her. Not to mention her newfound mother wasn't exactly giving her room to process everything.

It hadn't escaped Valencia's attention that Nattalie was obviously trying not to be near Anderson. Every time Lilian suggested they take a picture together, Nattalie insisted that Nate be in the picture too. Right between them. Again, Lilian was too preoccupied with creating the illusion of a happy family to notice. "Are we done yet?" Nate put his hand in the air like he was asking for permission to speak in school. Lilian looked annoyed at the question. "Oh, I guess so. Hey is everyone hungry? We can all go out to eat!" Before anyone could answer, Nick chimed in. "How about we just have dinner here?" The twins looked shocked at the invitation. Was he really inviting his ex-wife to dinner as a family? Even Lilian was shocked.

"Umm… are you sure Nick? You don't mind?"

"No, it'll be a good chance for you to meet Toni."

She tried her best not to let him see the disappointment on her face. "Sure. That's perfect." The twins stood with their mouths gaped, trying to figure out just what their dad was doing.

Valencia raised her hand to get Nick's attention. "Well I can help with dinner ya'll. I love to cook!" Before Nick could even say yes, she was making a bee line for the front door. After about thirty minutes it was apparent why she was so eager to help. Lilian kept popping into the kitchen trying to give motherly advice on preparing the food and properly setting a table. All to which both Valencia and Nattalie rolled their eyes. They just kept preparing the food as they had both done many times before without Lilian's help. Finally, she got the point and left the kitchen. Valencia walked over to Nattalie.

"Is she always like this?" I mean I don't wanna be rude. I know she's your…. Well, our mom. She's just……."

"Too much?"

"Yes! That's it! She's just too much!"

They both laughed together as they tossed the salad. "Ok the chicken is in the oven. We'll wait a few to put the rice on." Nattalie said while looking at her watch to start timing the chicken. "Hey how 'bout some sweet potatoes instead of rice? Do you have any?" Valencia had the cutest southern accent. Nattalie pointed to the pantry with a grin on her face. "Look in there. I think we do." They began to talk as they sat slicing the sweet potatoes. Mostly it was Valencia asking questions. Nattalie didn't mind though. She realized she must have a lifetime of questions. She asked about how they grew up and what vacations they took. What kinds of movies did they watch and had they ever had pets. Seemingly unimportant questions. But after a minute it seemed like maybe she was piecing together a life that she missed out on.

"Can I ask you something else Nattalie? You don't have to tell me but…"

"It's okay. What is it?"

"Why did your mom… I mean our mom… I mean...Why doesn't she live here with you? I mean I know she and your dad are divorced but... why does she live away from you all?"

Nattalie sat down her knife and wiped her hands on the kitchen towel that lay on the counter. Slowly she began to tell her sister the whole story. She told her about her birth father and the baby their mom lost in high school. How she left them to chase after an adolescent fantasy and now she was trying to fix it by bringing us together. As is if they were supposed to forget the pain she caused. Valencia sat in shock at what she was hearing. She had received a much more watered-down version of events. All she knew was that her mother had her in high school and was forced to give her up for adoption because she was so young. She knew nothing of another sibling or that she had abandoned Nathan and Nattalie to be with her father. Who was this woman? She thought to herself. She had come to California from Georgia with this stranger trying to find what she had been missing. "Valencia, I'm sorry. I shouldn't have told you all of that. I guess I'm still mad about it in a way." Valencia reached across the counter to grab Nattalie's hand. "You don't have to be sorry about a thing." Nattalie then looked down at Valencia's forearm and noticed a large bruise. "Oh my God. How did you get that?" She asked in a very concerned voice. Valencia quickly pulled her arm away and began to arrange the sweet potatoes in the pan.

"It's nothing. I'm super clumsy ya know."

"Well how did you hurt yourself?"

"I told you I'm clumsy. Always have been actually."

Nattalie felt something was wrong but didn't want to dig too deep. They were sisters but still strangers. So, they continued preparing dinner in silence.

With everyone now seated at the dining room table, the silence continued. Only the sounds of forks and knives against the plates were heard at first. Toni sat next to Nick and Lilian made it a point to sit directly on the opposite side of him. Nick scooted his chair just a little closer to Toni. "Oh, so we can have kids together, but I can't sit close to you? Is that it Nick?" Lillian snapped as if insulted. "Hey how's everyone's chicken?" Nattalie interrupted. They all began to nod in approval. "It's great. Who made the sweet potatoes?" Anderson asked. "Oh, that would be Valencia."

Nattalie answered. "I'm definitely gonna need a second helping of that." Nate added. "Well I thought we would all go for a walk afterwards or maybe catch a movie?" Nick suggested. "I don't really feel much like a family outing dad." Nattalie said. "Well how about the rest of you? You up for it?" Everyone shrugged their shoulders and nodded, okay. "Great, I'll call for the show times and we'll pick." Nick finished the last of his meal and left the table. They all sat looking awkwardly at each other. "You know you could make an effort to spend some time with your mother. I'm only here for a short time you know." Lillian snapped at Nattalie.

"Well you know if you were really concerned about spending time with us you wouldn't have left us to begin with!"

"Don't you speak to me like that! I'm still your mother!"

"You obviously didn't want that job, so you quit!"

"I did what I had to do! You don't understand what I was going through! How dare you judge me!"

"Now that's enough!" Nate shouted.

"Yes, please don't do this here. We can all sit and talk about it together." Toni tried desperately to be the peace maker.

"This is none of your business. These are me and Nicks kids!"

"What's going on?"

Nick came back into the dining room to an angry ex-wife and his daughter and girlfriend on the verge of tears. Nattalie got up from the table and went to her room.

"That's it. I was trying to make this pleasant for everyone, but you can't act right for a full day!"

"Don't you blame me Nick. It's that smart mouth daughter of yours that started it."

"She's sixteen! She's a kid! A kid whose life has changed dramatically because of your choices Lillian. Did you ever think that maybe you should just talk to your children about how they feel?"

"No, see that's not it. This woman you brought here has turned my kids against me!"

"Oh, give me break mom!" Nate yelled.

"You can't stand to even consider that this situation is of your own making!"

Nick put his hand on Toni's shoulder and turned to speak to Valencia and Anderson.

"Valencia, Anderson I am so sorry you had to witness this. I know you were expecting a better visit. You are welcome in this house as long as you're in town."

"So, I guess I'm not welcome Nick?"

"No, you are not Lillian. You can go to your hotel and if your children want to see you, they are old enough to reach out to you themselves. I suggest you quit being so self-centered and consider their feelings for once."

"Why? They never consider mine."

"I'll call you a cab Lillian."

☐She then picked up her purse and sunglasses to wait outside. Her pride and stubbornness were as strong as ever.

Three days and no word from their mother. The twins decided to get back to the fun part of summer. Valencia and Nattalie were quickly growing fond of each other. Neither of them had ever had a sister before and were eager to learn about each other. After the dinner disaster they decided that Valencia should stay with them while she was in town. That way they could get to know each other. It was a great idea, except Anderson asked if he could stay as well. Nattalie made sure to be joined at the hip with Valencia and Nate stayed on Anderson's heels.

It was the final week of their stay and all had actually gone well. They had somehow managed to enjoy themselves with no drama. Nattalie was almost comfortable around Anderson again. They even found themselves laughing at the same jokes. She figured maybe he was sorry and wanted to be friends. Desperately she wanted to forget and move on without fear of being in the same room with him. So, she decided to pretend it never happened and end the week well.

The six of them crowed into the old van and headed to ride the horse trails as a last outing before Valencia and Anderson's plain left in two days.

"Hey, have you guys heard from mom this week?"

"Uhh… she called late last week. She's supposed to meet Valencia and I at the airport Saturday morning."

"I wonder☐ what she's been doing this whole time."

No one had seen her since that last dinner. But no one was about to worry about it either. They all had the best time that day. And as they pulled up at home that evening, Nattalie felt like she could truly move on, forgive and forget.

Nick kissed Toni goodbye in the driveway and headed into the house.

"Hey dad."

"I'm gonna go play some football tonight at the park. Is that cool?"

"Yea that's fine son. Wish I had your energy."

"Let's go Anderson…"

"No thanks man. I'm pretty tired."

"Can I come and watch?" Valencia asked.

"Only groupies come to watch the guys play football."

"Well I ain't no groupie little brother."

"I guess it's okay. Just remember you are my sister. If anyone tries to hit on you, let me know."

"Whatever."

She rolled her eyes and smiled as they walked out the door. Anderson waved to Nate as he headed toward the patio where Nattalie was sitting and reading a book. At first, he paused and watched him. Something in him wanted to stay home instead. But he thought about the good day they had and decided he was being overprotective. Then he left. Soon after, Nick came onto the patio.

"Hey guys, I'm gonna go over to Toni's for a while."

"But you just said goodbye to her dad."

"Yes, but we decided earlier that we would have some alone time later. So, goodnight guys."

"Goodnight."

□Nattalie continued reading her book. She thought it strange that Anderson would want to sit on the patio in silence while she read. He began looking over his shoulder at the patio door. Fidgeting with his hands, rubbing the backs of them back and forth. She tried to continue reading but couldn't help but be distracted by his apparent uneasiness. He suddenly got up from his seat and went into the house. Nattalie sighed, feeling relieved that he had left. An hour or so had gone by and it was getting dark. She closed her book and went back into the house. As she opened her bedroom door, there was Anderson sitting on her bed, drinking a bottle of brandy.

Sweat was pouring down from his head and his eyes were blood shot. She felt a sudden panic grip her and she was frozen at the door. "What are you doing?" She asked with a quiver in her voice. Anderson took another drink as his body swayed slightly from side to side. "I'm waiting on you cuz." He grinned as his eyes seemed to peer right into her. Everything in her was screaming "get out!" She turned to run, and he leaped from the bed after her. She made it as far as the kitchen before he grabbed her. "HELP!!" She screamed and screamed. "God help me!" She kicked and struggled against him. He finally with all his might back handed her across the face and she collapsed on the kitchen floor. He knelt down near her as she struggled to get up. Then whispered in her ear, "There is no God." She sobbed as he picked her up and dragged her to her bedroom. He tried to force her to drink but she refused. So, he hit her again. "Why are you doing this to me?" He ripped her shirt open and grabbed both her arms. "Don't you get it?! The last time I felt normal was when you were with me!!" He got up and locked her bedroom door. "I've been a prisoner for most of my life!! Always a caretaker and never just a kid or even a person. When you came last winter, I felt like I was more than just my Mother's on call nurse." He began to undo his pants. "Please don't do this, please. We're family." She pleaded with him; her face wet with tears as he smiled at her. "Yes, we are, and you promised you'd be there for me." With those words he forced himself on her. It was like a thousand knives cutting through her body. Until she felt nothing but numb.

The sounds of shutting doors and running water woke Nattalie up the next morning. She hadn't left her room all night. She was afraid to be seen. No mirror was needed for her to know that her sore face was bruised. She could hear the shower in the hall bathroom running. How would she get to the bathroom herself without being seen? Anderson had taken a shower before everyone got home the night before and left her right where she was. As soon as she heard the bathroom door open and another door shut. She shot up out of bed as quickly as possible, ran to the bathroom and locked the door. Her face wasn't as badly bruised as she supposed, but still noticeable. She scrambled through drawers to find makeup. She didn't wear it all the time except when she and Kelsey were dressed up to go hang out. When she found the tube of chestnut brown foundation, she clutched it tight and began to cry. Her mind started pondering thoughts of drowning herself in the bathtub, rather than face her family and try to pretend everything was the same as it had always been. The pain of the hot shower water beating against her skin revealed more bruises and scratches from the night. She was terrified of having to look on his face. There were still three more days before he was supposed to leave. That was too long.

After taking time to cover her bruises, she darted back to her bedroom and locked the door. There was a note on her pillow. It was from Anderson.

My Nattalie,

I really am sorry if I hurt you, but you have to know that I love you. You are my blood and we are connected forever. I will always find my way back to you. All life is a search for pleasure, and I have found my pleasure in you.

Anderson

Her hands shook as she read his words. She reluctantly left her room to find her dad leaving the driveway with Anderson. Nate walked up behind her as she stared out the living room window. She jumped as he touched her shoulder.

"Sheesh Nate. You scared me!"

"What's gotten into you this morning?" He asked, confused at her reaction.

"Nothing, it's nothing. Where are dad and Anderson going?"

"Oh, he's going to Moms' hotel until they leave Saturday. He said he already told you goodbye."

Nate watched them drive off while eating an apple. Nattalie thought about his note and began to tear up. Would he be back? Would he really always find his way back to her? Nate was again confused at her reaction.

"Why are you crying Nattie? Did he tell you goodbye?"

□ "Yea……. he did."

How dark the next few days seemed. Her own room had become a tomb where her peace had been buried. She washed her sheets but the stain of what happened was still on it. Nattalie couldn't sleep. She woke up in the middle of the night swearing she could smell liquor in the air. His words kept repeating in her head. *"There is no God."*

She began to wonder if he was right. How could God let her be hurt like this? All the songs she learned as a kid about how Jesus loved her, seemed like fairytales. But if there is no God then was this really wrong? Was Anderson right? Is life just a pleasure hunt? Her thoughts consumed her, and nothing was making sense. Valencia had noticed her sudden distance the past couple of days and decided to find out what was wrong. "Hey lil sis." Valencia knocked on Nattalie's bedroom door and poked her head inside.

"Can I come in?"

"Sure." She sat up in bed and scooted over so Valencia could sit down.

"Well, I leave tomorrow hun. We haven't talked much the past couple of days. Thought I'd check on ya."

"Yea. I'm sorry. Just had a lot on my mind."

"Does that bruise on your face have anything to do with it?" Nattalie threw her hand up to her face to cover it. "It's okay hun, I won't tell, I understand."

"I don't think you do."

Valencia pulled Nattalie's hand away from her face. "Before I came here, I left my boyfriend of 3 years. He used to hit me, among other things…. Well the last time I was done. I decided I wanted better. That's part of the reason I agreed to come here with Lilian. I wanted to start over and possibly connect with family. Maybe even just move away."

"Do you think you'd want to live here with us? What about your adoptive parents?"

"They passed away some time ago. They were in their fifties when they adopted me."

She gave a little chuckle. "Listen I don't know who did that to you, but you deserve better. Hurting someone is never right." Nattalie began to cry and the two of them hugged each other tight.

"Please stay Valencia. Nate and I really like having you around."

"You know what. If I can find a decent job here, I'll come back." Nattalie smiled. "Really? You mean it?"

"I mean it sis."

They spent that last evening talking like sisters. They even kicked Nate out when he tried to join in. The room seemed a little less dark with her there.

The Long Fall Down

A month into their junior year in high school and things were finally feeling somewhat normal again. Nattalie had three classes with Kelsey and the same lunch period as Nate. All she needed was to get back to a routine and try to forget that summer ever happened. Except for Valencia. She talked to her almost every day since she left. Her resume was updated, and she was looking for work in California so she could relocate from Georgia. As close as she and Nate were, it was fun having a sister around.

Nate and Nattalie found a grassy spot to eat lunch in the courtyard of the school.

"Are you gonna audition for the fall play this year?" Nate asked.

"Nah, I don't think so. I have a killer biology class. If I don't buckle down this year, I'm gonna fail it. No time for extra stuff. Why did you ask?"

"Mom called asking if you were in a play this year. I guess she wanted to come."

"Well I'm definitely not doing it now."

"I feel bad sometimes though. Like…. she is our mom. Even if she is a selfish attention hog."

Nattalie just didn't want to be bothered with any talk of their mother. She was the reason they had to go to Minnesota in the first place. Anderson never could've done what he did if she hadn't moved away. Nate could tell she was getting upset by the way she began to press her lips together tight.

"Next subject. You want an ice cream Nattie cake?"

She giggled a little. "Yes! Hurry up and get me one!"

He ran to get her a chocolate crunch bar from the ice cream vending machine. As much as she wanted it. She felt nauseated as soon as she took the first bite.

"Ewww. I don't feel so good."

"Are you okay?"

Just then Nattalie turned to vomit in the grass. "You gotta go to the nurse sis." He held her hair as she continued to throw up. Kelsey was coming through the courtyard when she saw Nattalie.

"Hey! What's wrong with her Nate?"

"I don't know. She must've eaten something bad."

"I'll take her to the nurse."

☐Kelsey helped her up and led her to the nurse's office.

Later that afternoon, Nattalie was home in bed. Her dad had taken off work to come get her and Toni was on her way to see how she was doing.

"Hey pumpkin. I called Dr. Clayton's office and he can see you in the morning."

"No dad, I'm feeling much better. I have a quiz tomorrow I can't miss."

Nick wasn't sure he should cancel the appointment but decided he'd give it another day or so.

"Okay, but if you're still sick tomorrow, you're going. No argument."

☐ "Okay Dad."

Over the next few weeks, Nattalie's favorite foods became her worst enemy. She didn't want to go to the doctor. She tried her best to hide when something made her sick. She always felt better after throwing up. It seemed to be breakfast stuff mostly. While getting dressed one morning she noticed that her jeans were much more snug than usual. Assuming maybe they shrunk in the dryer, she just put on a dress instead.

"Nattie! Valencia is on the phone for you!"

"Just bring me the cordless phone silly!" He tossed it into her bedroom.

"Hey sis, what's up?"

"I got a job! That's what's up!" They both began screaming with joy over the phone.

"When do you start?"

"In three weeks! I can't wait. I have a real good feeling about this." Nattalie was so excited she forgot all about her nausea.

"Me too! Hey, I gotta get going to school sis, but call me later?"

"You bet. Bye!"

The doorbell rang and rang. "Does anyone live here?" Nick shouted from his bedroom. "Get the door!" Nattalie and Nate rushed to the door. They were both running late. Nate opened the door to find Kelsey looking quite annoyed.

"Sorry Kelsey. I couldn't find anything to wear."

"Are you serious? As much as we shopped all summer.... Whatever. Let's go."

They hurried off down the street. Good thing the school was only a ten-minute walk. "So, what's up with you lately?" Kelsey asked as Nattalie fidgeted with her dress. "Uh… nothing. Just feeling weird. I probably need vitamins or something." Kelsey rolled her eyes. "You need therapy or something." She said with a chuckle.

"What? Why would you say that?"

"I mean, you've been in a mood for weeks. You hardly ever wanna hang since school started. I thought you were mad at me for a minute."

"I'm not mad at you Kelsey. I'm just..."

"Hey Natt, what's going on? You gotta tell me."

"It doesn't matter...let's just get to school." Nattalie wiped the tears that were welling up in her eyes and continued walking. ☐Kelsey knew enough about Nattalie to know that trying to force her to talk was useless. So, they continued on to school.

Two weeks past and Nattalie felt she had finally gotten past whatever stomach bug had been plaguing her. There was a football game at their school that she had no interest in. But Kelsey liked to boyfriend hunt. So, she convinced her to go with her. It was a Friday night and she really didn't have anything else to do. Hiding her sudden weight gain from Nate and her Dad had become a fulltime job. It didn't get past Kelsey though. Kelsey loaded up on snacks from the concession stand and met Nattalie in the bleachers.

"Ewww...what's that smell?"

"It's just Nachos girl… What's wrong with you? You pregnant or something?"

"Oh my God!"

Just then, it hit Nattalie like a ton of bricks. She shot up and hurried down the bleachers. "Wait! Where are you going Natt!" Kelsey left her snacks and chased after her. They were almost to the street before she caught up to her. "Stop! Wait a second!" She grabbed her arm and she jerked it away. Nattalie stopped and sat on the sidewalk. She began to cry. Kelsey sat down next to her and held her hand. After a few moments of tears and silence Kelsey carefully spoke.

"Natt, are you pregnant?"

"I don't know. But I could be...why didn't I see it before? I could be..."

Kelsey got up and reached for Nattalie's hand to pull her up.

"Welp.... We'd better find out. The drug store up the street is still open. Let's get a pregnancy test."

"I can't go in there."

"Fine, I'll get it. But you owe me."

It was too risky to take the test to her house. So, they decided to go to Kelsey's house. Her parents were out for the evening. Kelsey ran to the drug store and made it back to find Nattalie sitting on her front porch.

"I got it!"

"Okay. Let's get this over with."

"We'll do it the hall bathroom."

Three minutes for the results felt like three hours as they sat outside the bathroom waiting for the timer to go off. When the timer went off, they both went in to see. The positive sign on the plastic applicator seemed to scream at her. □Nattalie was so stunned she couldn't even cry. Of all the ways she could've imagined her Friday night to turn out. She never thought she would end the night pregnant.

Home was the last place she wanted to go. Sleeping in that bed where she had been so horribly violated. Struggling to pretend that everything was just as it had always been. It was all too much. She walked around her block for over an hour. Trying to come up with a solution, but nothing came. Abortion wasn't an option; she had no money. Even if she did, no one would agree to take her. Her dad and brother would demand to know who the father was on top of it all. The only choice she had was to tell the truth before things got any messier than they already were. She took a deep breath and did something she hadn't done in a long time. She prayed.

> *"Dear God, I don't know if you're there anymore or if you ever were. But if you are, please help me. I can't face this alone. So, if Anderson is wrong and you're real then you gotta show up now."*

She wiped her tears and headed home to tell the truth and unburden herself. One thing she never doubted was her dad and brothers love for her. Even more, she had a sister who would be there soon.

Before walking into the house, she paused to go over just what she was going to say. Walking into the living room the first thing she saw was Toni and her dad sitting on the couch. Toni looked like she had been crying and was fidgeting with a tissue in her hand. Nate was leaned against the wall with his arms folded and head down. They all looked up as she entered the room.

"What's going on?"

"Why don't you sit down sweetie?"

"Sit? No, I don't wanna sit. What's wrong?"

Nate walked over to her, trying not to cry. Her eyes were fixed on his face. Waiting for his lips to part with whatever the news was. "Nattie, Valencia is dead." The feeling in her legs disappeared and she slumped to the floor. Nate pulled her back up and helped her to the couch.

"How....HOW?"

"It was her boyfriend. Police say it looks like they got in a fight. She ran but he chased her down with his car. He hit her in the middle of the street. She was trying to leave. Guess the relationship had been abusive for a long time."

"No, no, no!!"

Nattalie ran from the living room and out the back door. Nate chased after her. He knew where she was going, to the roof. By the time she got to the top Nate was already climbing his way up behind her.

"Nattie, you shouldn't be up here while you're this upset."

"Just leave me alone! Nothing matters!"

She slipped on a loose shingle and caught herself. "Oh God Natt, please don't fall. Just come down with me please. We'll get through this!"

"God? WHAT GOD?! If there's a God, why did mom leave? Why is Valencia dead? Why am I …… AHHHHHHH."

She slipped again and began to tumble down the roof. "NOOO!!" Nate screamed out for her. When he got to the ground, she was unconscious.

Unconscious

Nick, Nate, and Toni stood around the doctor in the waiting room of the ICU.

"I'm very sorry Mr. Blythe but your daughter is in a coma. She's suffered a brain injury and there is significant swelling."

"How long will my daughter be that way? Will she wake up?"

"There's no way to tell at the moment. We've lowered her body temperature to prevent more swelling and allow her brain to heal. Unfortunately, we were unable to save the baby."

"Wait, what? What baby? There's no baby."

"So, what are you saying Doc□? My sister is pregnant?"

"Was, pregnant. About eight weeks or so. It was too early in the pregnancy to survive a fall like that."

Nate began to cry in anger. He couldn't understand why she didn't tell him. Had something changed between them? Nothing was making any sense at all. "You can go in and see her now but family only." Toni gently rubbed Nicks back. "I'll just wait here Love." Nick turned and kissed her cheek with tears rolling down his. He and Nate then walked down the hall of the ICU to see Nattalie.

One Week Later

The only thing more depressing than the sight of his sister hooked up to machines, was the food in the hospital cafeteria. Nate hadn't been to school in a week. He and Nick were practically living at the hospital. When he just couldn't stomach the cafeteria food, he turned to the vending machines. That's where Lilian found him the day she showed up. Fighting with a vending machine for a candy bar. "You know you should have a healthier breakfast son." She said as she walked up behind him. He turned quickly at the sound of her voice.

"Mom…. you're here."

"You looked surprised son." He reached down to grab the candy bar from the machine.

"I just figured you'd be busy with Valencia's funeral and all."

"Well I was. That's what took me so long to get here."

"Yea… well it's not as if it would've mattered. She doesn't know any of us are here. You may as well have stayed where you were."

"Don't say that Nate. She's my daughter……. they are both my daughters. I wanted to be there for them both! I tried to fix it! I just wanted……"

☐She sobbed. As much as Nate wanted to hate her and care less about her tears. All he could feel was pity. He had only known Valencia a short time and was hurt at her passing. His mother had lost and found her. Only to lose her again. He put his candy bar down and held his mother as she cried and cried on his chest. It seemed like ages since they had been that close.

Nick and Toni went for a morning walk on the hospital grounds. Nick would've been happy to stay in Nattalie's room just watching his baby girl, but Toni insisted he get some air. After a few silent, slow laps around the courtyard, they spotted a bench and sat down. "I saw Lilian come in a little while ago." Toni broke the silence. Nick just nodded at her words. "She was looking for Nate and I told her where he was." Nick rolled his eyes, "Why didn't she go see Nattalie first? I shouldn't even ask. Probably some selfish reason knowing her." Toni shrugged. "I don't know sweetie. Maybe she wanted to see how he was holding up. Maybe she needed a little support before she saw Nattalie in that condition. She's been through a lot this week ya know." Nick sighed. He knew she was right. It had been a rough week for them all. Maybe she needed to lay eyes on the only child she had that could look back at her. It amazed him how gracious and understanding Toni could be. She was a rock. She never gave into the drama and always tried to keep things in perspective. "Thank you..." He said as he grabbed her hand.

"For what sweetie?"

"For being here… I…. I feel like I'm in a bad dream. I'm with my kids every day. How did I not know she was pregnant?"

"I thought I knew my kids. I thought we were getting better as a family. What did I do wrong Toni?? What did I do?"

"You've done your best as a father, Nick. She's an individual. Separate from you and she's growing up. Besides, we don't even know what happened yet. I do know that I am not going to let you blame yourself." She gently turned his face toward hers. "We will get through this. All of it." He began to gather himself and thought to do something he hadn't done in a while.

"Toni, can we pray? I mean together for Nattalie."

"Of course, we can sweetie." They took hands and Nick with his heart wide open, talked to God.

☐ "Lord, I don't know what's going on, but you do. I barely think I know my own daughter, but you do. Please…. help her. Whatever is going on is obviously outside my ability to fix…Amen."

Nate and Lilian sat next to Nattalie's hospital bed. It was strange to see his mother sit so quietly. Almost in shock. After about twenty minutes had gone by, Lilian began to hum. Nate really didn't pay much attention to what she was humming until he recognized the tune. It was the bath time song she used to sing to them as children. *"I'm a little ducky in the water. SPLASH, SPLASH, SPLASH! SPLASH, SPLASH, SPLASH! I'm a little ducky in the water ……"* Over and over she hummed the tune and sang the simple words that had stuck in his memory all these years. That was one of their fondest memories. She never minded the splashing of the water. She thought it was hilarious how they'd splash their hardest with the lyrics of the song. She was all the world to them. As quickly as the memory brought a smile to his face, it was gone. Replaced with the question of, why? Why did she change? Why weren't they enough to make her smile anymore? Why weren't they enough reason for her to stay? He got up and walked out into the hall. He couldn't take hearing that tune anymore.

Lilian didn't want to leave Nattalie but needed to make sure Nate was okay. She kissed her face. "I'll be back Nattie." Then went after Nate. He wasn't in the hall, so she went toward the elevators. He was just stepping on when she came running up behind him. "Wait! Stop Nate!" She barely made it onto the elevator before the door closed.

"Where are you going?"

"I need some air that's all."

"Listen, I know this is hard, but we can't get through this without each other."

"Oh really? Well you left us to get through a lot of things by ourselves, so I think we'll be fine. Thanks." The doors opened and he all but ran out of there. "Please Nate let's just talk. I need you!" That was enough to make his blood boil. He stopped and turned around in the middle of the hospital lobby. Looking her straight in the face.

"You need me? YOU NEED ME! What about when we needed you?!"

"Okay… I know you're upset but we're still in a hospital. Don't yell."

"You think I care right now?! I was feeling so bad for you a while ago. You've lost a lot. But you're still the same selfish person that ran out on us."

"That's not true Nate, it's not true. I know I left, and I can never make up for that but I'm trying to be better. I need you but I want to be there for you too. Can't we be there for each other? I just want to be your mom again."

At these words Nate walked out into the courtyard. Trying to believe her at that moment was just too much of a stretch.

Another week had gone by and Lilian decided to go to Georgia to attend Valencia's funeral. Her stomach was in knots the day she left. She spent the night before in the hospital with Nattalie just in case she woke up☐. Waiting until the last possible minute to leave before she would be late for her flight. "I love you baby. I'll be back soon; I promise I promise." She said in a whisper, almost as if she were pleading for Nattalie to believe her. After she kissed her forehead, she left to bury her first daughter.

Nothing about the funeral was normal. Instead of an intimate gathering of family and friends to say goodbye to a loved one. It was a media circus with reporters and cameras everywhere. Valencia's murder had been the biggest news to ever hit that little town. There were still a lot of people in Valencia's life who weren't aware that she was adopted. Let alone knew that she had recently come in contact with her biological family. Lilian felt like a stranger crashing a family reunion walking into the little church. Everyone seemed to know everyone in that town. So as soon as she walked in, she was drowning in whispers and curious stares. All of a sudden while standing in the line to view to body, she felt that knot in her stomach again. She began to sweat and became short of breath. She looked for a place to sit quickly and rushed out of the line. Her hands shook. She thought maybe it wasn't really Valencia in the casket. Maybe this whole thing was a mistake. She wasn't really out of time. There was still a chance to fix what she had made such a mess out of. As she watched the family members one by one pass the casket sobbing and a few collapsing having to be carried away. She lost her nerve. She couldn't go up there. At that moment, a rather large woman came and sat next to her. "How ya holding up darling?" The woman asked in a very kind and concerned voice. "Uhhhh…. I don't know really." Lilian answered. She wasn't really sure why this woman was speaking to her at all. The woman put her hand over Lilian's shaking hands to steady them.

"I know who you are darling."

"You do?"

"Mmm Hmmm. You're Val's mother. She told me all about you after she got back from California."

"She did?"

"Yes, she was quite excited about meeting her family. Although I might've guessed ya'll was related. Mmmm. She sho is the spittin' image of you."

"May I ask how you knew her?"

"Chile she practically grew up in my house. I was her second-grade teacher and she and my daughter were friends. After her adoptive parents passed away, I took it on myself to see after her. She was grown but I wanted her to know she still had family."

While speaking she had begun to cry. Lilian grabbed tighter to her hand. She wasn't the only one who had lost a daughter.

"What's your name?"

"I'm sorry, I'm Ruth Covington. You can call me Ruthy."

"Ruthy, I can't go up there alone. Will you come with me?"

"I'm glad you asked. I was having trouble getting up the nerve myself."

They both gave a little laugh and came back into the aisle to view the body. The few feet that they walked felt like a hundred miles of dread. When they reached the casket, a surge of heat shot through Lilian's body. She shook her head rapidly trying to remove the image from her sight. Valencia was the very image of Nattalie in that casket. Her legs suddenly weren't there anymore, and the room was upside down. A deacon came over to help pick Lilian up off the floor. Once she was on her feet, Ruthy helped her back to her seat. Lilian never heard a word that was said from the pull pit that day. All she kept seeing was Nattalie inside that casket. The resemblance was too much for her to handle. She looked up at the preacher and the cross in the background of the choir stand. In that moment she became angry with God. She was trying to fix all she had done, and it just kept falling apart. Why would a forgiving God let it all fall apart in such a horrible way?

The reporters were relentless. They stayed buzzing around the Cemetery, trying to get a statement from anyone they could. Although it hurt that no one else recognized her as Valencia's mother, Lilian was glad not to be getting followed by cameras. The repass wasn't far from the cemetery so she decided to walk there and clear her head along the way. She had no interest in staying, she only went to say a proper goodbye to Ruthy who had been so kind to her. Ruthy noticed Lilian slowly coming up the walkway to the house. She waved for her to come onto the porch where she was sitting with some other family. "I was hoping you would come." Ruthy grabbed Lilian and hugged her as if she had been family all along. "Well I only came to say goodbye to you. I have to get back to California." Lilian turned her eyes toward the ground. "My other daughter is in a coma." Ruthy gently grabbed her hand and sat her down next to her on an old wicker sofa.

"Oh child... I'm so sorry."

"It's okay. I just have to be there. Maybe if I had been there for Valencia, this wouldn't have happened."

Ruthy, leaned back with a smirk on her face, shaking her head.

"What are you smirking at?"

"Girl, you really think that you can control everything don't you?"

"Well I ......"

"You didn't have nothing to do with Valencia's choice in that man."

"But if I had been there, if I had raised her…."

"What would've happened? Do you know for sure?"

"No, I don't know for sure."

"No, you don't. You know I knew your mother. She was a hard woman and I know she made you give that baby up and you resented her for it. But she did what she thought was best for you at the time. Valencia had a good life growing up. Parents who loved her, a good education. Friends and family. In the end she had to make her own decisions in life and that remains the same no matter who raised her."

Lilian felt strange. Almost relieved at her words. She began to giggle to herself.

"Child are you alright?"

"I'm fine... really. I mean I have so many regrets. I've tried to fix them all, but I just keep failing."

"You gon' drive yourself plum crazy trying to go back in time to fix everything. You'll probably end up with a bigger mess!"

Ruthy put her plump arm around Lilian and gave her a little squeeze.

"Forgive yourself child. Then after you do that, just move forward. You still have kids that need you even if they don't think they do."

"How did you know?"

"Oh, I had a feeling. I've been you before and had to learn some hard lessons. It's never too late to turn back though. God still loves you and he's faithful even when we are not. Go on now. Go see about your daughter. What's done here is done."

Lilian hugged Ruthy tight then went on her way back to California.

On the plane ride back, Lilian thought about many things. She really had made a mess. For the first time in years she was pointing the finger at herself. Her efforts to fix it all, were just about her. Empty was all she could feel, and her mind couldn't conjure a plan to make her whole again.

Back at the hospital things were looking better. The swelling had gone down in Nattalie's brain and Nate had even returned to school. Nick had prayed more than he had since Lilian left. He even dusted off his Bible and dared to read it. Sometimes even out loud to Nattalie. "Hey dad." Nate walked into the hospital room and sat his book bag on the floor. "Any change?" Nick shook his head and sat his coffee on the nightstand.

"Well, I heard mom is supposed to be back today. Apparently, she talked to Toni."

"She called Toni?"

"Mmm, Hmmm…. Yup. I guess she figured your phone would be off here." Just then Toni walked into the room. "Did I hear my name?" Nick stood up. "Are you okay? Was she rude to you?" Toni giggled. "No, no. She was fine. She'll be here tomorrow." Nick looked over at the Bible on his chair. "Well, that's one miracle." They all began to laugh. "Whatever dad. If it makes you feel better. I wish she'd just stay away." Nick sighed and put his hand on Nates shoulder.

"Son, you don't mean that."

"But dad…"

"No son. I can't fix things between you and your mom. She banged that up pretty darn good. But you need each other. The sooner you both realize that, then you both can start healing……. Son?"

Nate had looked up to see Nattalie's hand twitching and her eyelids fluttering. "Dad look." Nick turned around just as her eyes slowly □began to open.

Imagine waking up from a nightmare but feeling no relief that it was over. Because when your eyes opened you found that you had been plunged from one nightmare into another. This was just how Nattalie felt the morning she regained consciousness. Swept into another nightmare. A doctor and a few nurses gathered around her bedside. She could see and hear them but had no power to speak because of the tubes that were still down her throat. When her family was allowed to be alone with her after what seemed like days of testing, blood work and doctor lingo she couldn't understand, all she could do was cry. Her father, mother and brother were all there the next morning. She was never happier to see their faces but couldn't shake the despair that sat on her chest like a heavy stone. "Hey little girl. We're all here... we're all here." Nick was fighting back streams of tears and losing the battle. "The doctor said that yucky tube can come out. You're recovering so well......" His words got caught in the lump in his throat. Finally, he just broke down and sobbed. "Dad's just happy Nattalie... we all are." Nate said as he fought back tears of his own. Lilian hadn't said a word up to this point. She stared at her daughter's face but kept having flash backs of Valencia in the casket. She wanted to wipe the image from her mind, but she couldn't. She slowly leaned over to kiss her forehead and whispered in her ear. "I love you sweetheart and I am so, so, sorry." Nattalie turned her head to look at her mother. She wasn't sure before if the word "sorry" had been in her mother's vocabulary. She needed to look her in the face. "I'm here for good. I promise I'll never leave you again." Since she had been whispering, Nate only caught the last part of what she said. He wanted to ☐tell her to quit trying to get her hopes up. "You know you'll leave at the first sight of a good man or money", he thought to himself. But he kept quiet. He hadn't seen his sister and his mother stare so intently at each other since they were small. It was heartwarming and yet heart breaking to think how another disappearance by her could destroy them. Still he kept quiet.

The next day the nurse came in to take the feeding tube out. Nattalie had been rubbing her stomach all night. It wasn't bulging like it had been before her fall. It was flat just like before. No one had mentioned the pregnancy. She wondered if they knew or if she was even pregnant anymore. "Good day dear!" A very cheery nurse with short red hair came into the room. She approached the bed with the biggest smile Nattalie had ever seen on an actual person. "What was she so cheery about?" She thought. No sooner had she completed her thought, she didn't care about the nurses oversized smile anymore. That tube was coming out and now she could ask someone about what had been on her mind all night long. A second nurse came in to assist. She was far less cheery than the red headed nurse. She was short, plump and didn't smile at all. "Ok darling, just relax. This is gonna be uncomfortable coming out and you'll gag a little. But the good news is that you can try real food today!" Nurse red head was so darn nice it was near impossible to be upset or afraid. She made getting a feeding tube taken out almost sound fun. A few minutes later it was out and Nattalie was left with a sore throat and lips that felt like sandpaper. Her family had gone home to shower and change. It was good to have a little bit of quiet after nurse red head gave her the lunch options. Anderson was on her mind like a thick fog. His words had stuck in her head ever since the last time he raped her. "There is no God." She recalled Sunday school lessons about 'Noah's Ark' and 'Jonah and the Great Fish.' "Jesus loves me" was the first song she ever learned in church as a child. But it was all feeling like a lie. She grew sick at the memory of her attacker and a faint smell of liquor was in the air. At one point she had fallen asleep and woke up startled to see his face as she opened her eyes. "Am I going crazy?" She thought, as she wiped the sweat from her face. "Hey, hey look who's up." An excited Nate came into the room caring a bouquet of Gerber Daisies. Nick was right behind him with balloons and a box of chocolate turtles. They were all her favorite. "Hey guys." She said in a raspy voice. Her throat still felt dry and sore.

"What's all this Dad?"

"Well we don't know how much longer you'll be here we figured we'd spruce up this drab room."

Nick tied the balloons to a chair. "I hope it's not long. I don't want to stay here." Even though that was true, she did hope she got released soon. There was a dread about going home. Seemed like everything bad had happened there and she didn't know how to go "home." If home is where the heart is, like she'd heard in old movies, then she had no home. Her heart had only been hurt there and she didn't want to be hurt anymore.

While hurt was on her mind, she noticed that her mom wasn't there. "Is mom here?" Nate nodded his head. "She's gonna be here a lil later. Something she had to take care of this morning." Nattalie wasn't quite sure why but she wanted her mom there. She had dared to believe the words she spoke to her after she woke up. Now was the test to see if she really could be there for her. "Dad…" Nick looked up at his daughter whose eyes were filling with tears. She was touching her stomach. "Am I …… am I still?"

Nick got up and sat by her bed. "Sweety, they couldn't save ☐the baby. It was too early in the pregnancy to survive that fall." The mixed bag of emotions was over whelming. The sadness of losing the life she had so briefly carried and the relief of not having to carry Anderson's rape child were merging together. Creating a feeling that she didn't recognize, nor could she explain. All she knew was that she wasn't the same person anymore.

"Good morning Nattalie." The doctor came into the room just as Nick had arrived that morning. "We need to run some test today to take another look at your brain. The initial swelling was significant and after an injury like yours, the nerve cells may no longer send Information to each other like normal." Nattalie immediately had an image of her brain with little electric sparks that weren't firing off quite right. "We will also do a series of physical tests to see where your strength, coordination and mobility are." This concerned her a bit. While she attempted to eat a solid meal the evening before she had kept dropping her spoon. Her fingers couldn't quite grip the handle tight enough. "I'll send the nurses in to get started soon. Any questions?" They both shook their heads not really knowing if they should be asking anything else. "No, thank you doctor." He nodded and left the room. It was only nine o'clock in the morning and already she felt exhausted.

"Knock, knock!" Nurse red head came into her room the next morning with her usual upbeat greeting. "This lady just never has a bad day." Nattalie thought. "Okay darling, the doctor has ordered some test to see how you're doin' up there." She said gesturing toward Nattalie's head. Heading down the halls of the hospital Nattalie noticed nurse red head wore a silver cross around her neck. She hummed as she wheeled her in for the CT Scan. It was a tune that sounded familiar but Nattalie just couldn't put her finger on what it was. It was hymn, she knew that much.

After a morning of having the privacy of her brain invaded. It was time for the physical test. Nurse red head accompanied a physical therapist to help her get up and walk. She hadn't walked in over two weeks. Her legs felt like jelly and she didn't trust them to keep her off the ground when her feet hit the floor. "Take it slow Nattalie, you're doing great." Nurse red head said with a smile. Her legs wobbled as she struggled to take steps. Putting one in front of the other took a significant amount of concentration and finally she missed a step and fell down on the padded floor. "It's okay dear, it's okay." They both helped her up and continued with a series of other physical tests. Her normally caramel face was a deep burgundy. Caught somewhere between frustration, embarrassment, and determination. Nurse red head helped Nattalie back into the wheelchair.

"Alright, good job! Let's get you back to your room now. I bet you're hungry."

"Please, can I just sit in the chair by the window for a little bit? I don't wanna get back in that bed right now."

After returning to the room the hospital bed looked more like a prison than a bed. The sun was shining so brightly through the window, she thought maybe she would feel better if she could feel its warmth on her body. "I think that's a lovely idea. How about I help you back into bed after lunch?" Nattalie nodded. As soon as she was sure that she was a lone, she began to cry hard. She could hardly catch her breath in between sobs. Even sitting in the sun staring out at such a beautiful day, she could see no beauty. Only a cruel existence that made no sense at all. "What's the point of any of it?" She thought. "It's all just one big accident and a struggle to survive it ... but survive for what? Another hurt? Why did I even wake up?" Her thoughts fumbled between self-pity and despair. As she sank deeper and deeper a hand touched her shoulder. It startled her so badly she almost jumped out of the chair. "Mom..." Nattalie looked up to see her mother standing over her with a smile. It was very much like the smile she remembered when she and Nate were little. Gentle and bright. "Mommy…. why? □" She reached up to wrap her arms around her mom. Lilian didn't know how to respond or what exactly she was asking. She just hugged and kissed her. Assuring her that it was all going to be okay even though she wasn't quite convinced of it herself.

"After reviewing the results of the CT Scan and the report from the physical therapist I have to say that you're recovering quickly, and I'm pleased to see this." Nattalie looked up at the doctor with both eyebrows raised. Then looked at her parents whose reaction was about the same. Except Toni who just sat with a satisfied grin on her face.

"Wait but I fell during the physical test. I can barely hold my spoon while eating and..."

"The difficulties you are displaying aren't uncommon with traumatic brain injuries. But over all you are recovering well. Some people can't even talk or swallow after an injury like yours." They were all in a state of relief. Nate grabbed his sister's hand and kissed it.

"You will need to continue physical therapy after you're released at least three days a week."

"Released? I'm going home?"

"Indeed, you are. I want to get some blood work done before I officially release you but if all comes back good, you can go home day after tomorrow."

Still feeling mixed emotions about going home, Nattalie couldn't find words. "Thank you so much doctor for all you've done." Lilian shook the doctor's hand and he left the room.

Later that ☐night she was alone again. Her fears of going home were multiplied when she realized that no one had yet asked her about who the baby's father was. In fact, no one had pressed her about it at all. They were sure to bring it up once she was home. There wasn't a lie she could think of that would get her out of this. The truth was always a choice. But the truth would rip an even bigger hole in the family. Her mom was home and actually getting along with Toni. Even Nate seemed less frustrated when she was around. Telling the truth would only make things worse. She decided to eat her pain in silence. It was the only way to move forward without any more chaos. She stayed up most of the night thinking and looking at the moon. Wishing there was some way to make the night go by slower.

Not There Yet

"Good morning, I brought donuts. How's she feeling today?" Lilian asked Nick as she entered the house and took off her jacket.

"She's here. That's gotta be good enough for now. She really hasn't said much since we got home."

"It's probably best to let her be for now. But...."

"But what?"

"Well... I wanna know who. Who was she pregnant by? I've been afraid to ask Lily. I don't really know if it matters at this point."

"Of course, it matters. We don't want her sexually active at this age. If it's some boyfriend, we don't know about then..."

Lilian heard footsteps and figured it was Nate coming into the living room. "We'll talk later." She whispered.

"Hey, is Nattie up yet?"

"No son, we're trying to let her alone for a while."

"That's ridiculous! She doesn't need to be alone. She needs her family."

Nate walked over to the refrigerator, poured a glass of orange juice, and put a bagel on a paper towel with strawberry cream cheese. "We have donuts if you want Nate. I know you don't like bagels much." Lilian opened the box of donuts she brought in. "This is for Nattie, she hates donuts." With that, he marched off to his sister's room.

Nate approached Nattalie's bedroom door and heard a strange creaking sound coming from the room. He slowly cracked the door open and peeked inside. "Nattie... Nattie." He found her sitting in an old rocking chair, rocking herself back and forth. "Hey you're up... I brought you a bagel with strawberry cream cheese." He smiled as he handed it to her. A little smirk appeared on her face as she reached out for it, although she hadn't been hungry for days. Had it been her mom or dad who had come with food, she would've refused. But her twin always new just what she needed and just how to give it. "Have you talked to Kelsey since you've been home?" She shook her head with a mouth full of bagel.

"Toni said she asked about you every time she saw her."

"Why didn't she come to the hospital then?"

"I don't know Nattie. Seems weird."

"Whatever. Nothing matters anyway."

"Don't talk like that. You matter."

"Why? Why do I matter? Are you gonna give me some speech about self-worth Nate? Some sermon?"

"What's wrong Nattalie? Tell me!"

"I'm tired Nate, just forget it."

"Look, mom and dad may think you're too fragile to talk about it, but I don't. You can tell me the truth. Who were you pregnant by? I know you don't have a boyfriend. You would've told me. Did something bad happen?"

She was frozen in her seat. She wanted to tell him, but her tongue was stuck to the roof of her mouth. Her body shook and her breathing became labored.

"Nattie calm down. It's okay. You gotta tell me." "

"Please. If I tell you, you have to promise not to say anything to mom or dad. It'll just make things worse."

"I swear I won't."

Her palms became sweaty and. Her heart was beating in her throat. She put her head down as she spoke.

"Anderson."

 "Who did you say?"

She lifted her head, so her eyes met his. With tears streaming down her face. "Anderson." His mind immediately went back to the evening he left her alone with Anderson. He felt so uneasy leaving but couldn't quite put his finger on why. Then he thought of the trip to Minnesota. He hated the way Anderson looked at her. Nate's mind raced. "How could I not have seen it?" He thought. Nattalie sat up in the rocking chair. She had never seen her brother in such as state. "Nate, Nate are you okay? Nate say something!" He said nothing. He stood still with his chest heaving up and down like it was about to explode. A single tear ran down his cheek and he ran out of her bedroom. If only her legs were strong, she would've run after him. But all she could do was sit there and worry.

Shortly after Nate left, Lilian and Toni came into Nattalie's room.

"Is everything okay sweetie?"

"Nate just ran out of the house. What's wrong?"

"Nothing's wrong. Everything is fine. So, what, are the two of you a team now?" Lilian and Toni looked at each other.

"Umm we're just concerned about you." Toni said.

"We know this is hard…"

"Do you? Look, could you both just leave please?"

"Okay we'll leave but I'll check on you in a little while. Don't forget you have a physical therapy appointment in the morning."

☐Nattalie didn't reply. She was seeing little point in going to physical therapy. She was seeing little point to anything anymore.

The next morning Lilian helped Nattalie find something to wear. They barely spoke. Things were still awkward. Knowing that her mom wanted to ask the same question she'd answered for Nate the day before was making her feel anxious.

"Your brother said he wants to go with you to therapy. If that's okay with you."

"Yea. I need to talk to him anyway."

"Well I'm driving so your dad and Toni don't have to miss work."

"Why are you being so nice to them? Especially Toni. You hate her."

☐Lilian sat down on the bed next to her. "I don't hate her. I never hated her. I just blamed her. I blamed a lot of people for my own misery. But I can't anymore." She grabbed Nattalie's hand. "All that matters is that I take care of my kids and you have a mom you can count on." Nattalie wanted to pinch herself to make sure she was awake. "Maybe I'm still in the coma." She thought. Her mother hadn't been this warm and sweet since she was little. It was hard to know how to respond.

A friendly and very young-looking man came to the car with a wheelchair to help Nattalie inside. Nate jumped out of the car and all but pushed the young man out of the way. "I can get her inside. Thanks." Nate motioned him away from the car and helped Nattalie into the wheelchair. "What's wrong with you Nate? That was so rude." Nattalie felt embarrassed at his action. "Yes, son it was rude. That's his job to help patients." Nate didn't even respond to either of them. He just wheeled her toward the glass sliding doors. "Let's go so we're not late." Despite how irritated Nattalie was with Nate. She kept quiet. She hadn't spoken to him since she told him about Anderson. He disappeared for the rest of that day. She knew it was still heavy on his mind. Inside they were greeted by a tall muscular man with dark hair and deep olive skin. "Hello, I'm Zacharias.

I'm the physical therapist. You must be my new test subject." Nattalie paused to make sure she heard him correctly. "I'm just kidding." The man chuckled at his own joke. "Oh..." Nattalie and Lilian began to chuckle as well. Nate however unamused, glared at the man. "So, what's the plan? How are you gonna make her get better?" Nate said almost threateningly. Lilian grabbed his arm.

"Boy what is wrong with you? I'm so sorry sir, forgive my son. His sister's injury has him a bit on edge."

"I understand. I can tell you this. It's not going to be easy. There may be times of frustration in the process and even pain. But I'm committed to not giving up on you. You have to decide that you are committed to the process and not give up on it. Oh, and you can call me Zach." He smiled the nicest smile she'd seen since nurse red head. "So, you ready to get started?" Nattalie nodded her head almost reluctantly. The thought of more pain and more frustration didn't exactly sound comforting.

"Can my brother and mom stay with me?"

"Yea, that's not a problem. There's an area where they can sit."

They walked down the hall to the training room. It wasn't quite what Nattalie was expecting. She didn't think there would be other people there. Lilian and Nate took a seat in an area off to the side. No sooner than they had entered the room a frail looking blonde haired boy locked eyes with her. He was with another therapist doing some kind of stretches on the mat. She and Zach began with some routine exercises and test to see just how far she had to go. She stood with Zach's assistance, but her legs wobbled. He asked her to put one foot in front of the other. She was telling her foot to move forward but it wouldn't respond. She just wobbled there, fighting back tears. "Ok Nattalie, you can sit down." She flopped back into the wheelchair, sweating with her face flushed. Looking up she saw the blonde-haired boy staring at her again. At this point she was annoyed. She already felt self-conscious enough without some boy staring at her. The boy's session ended before hers and he even had the nerve to wink at her on the way out. Seeing that she was exhausted and frustrated, Zach ended their first session a few minutes early.

"That's enough for today. You did good girl."

"If that's what you call good I don't wanna see your bad patients."

☐ "Listen, this is a journey. Not a race. Just keep trying and you'll get there. Like I said, I won't give up. You just have to show up."

Weeks went by. Weeks of pain and days of small victories. Some days her dad and Toni would take her to therapy. The blonde boy didn't seem to pay as much attention to her when her dad or Nate were near. They both noticed his gaze and didn't care much for it. One particular day she noticed him having a considerable amount of trouble lifting a small dumbbell. She watched his fingers barely holding onto it. Trembling all the way through to his arm. He finally lifted it but didn't seem at all satisfied to have done so. "Nattalie, do you know what day it is?" Zach said with a huge smile on his face as he entered the training room. She shook her head to unlock herself from the boy.

"Uhhh... no. What day is it?"

"It's your ninetieth day of therapy."

"Is that good?"

"For the progress you've made, that's very good."

She wanted to be happy but something inside her just couldn't get excited about it. "What would learning to walk again mean anyway?" She thought. Nothing was ever going to be the same. Then Valencia suddenly came to her mind. She would never know her the way she had wanted to. Then she thought about her brother. He may never look at her the same again. She never got to explain exactly what happened with Anderson. All she knew was that they hadn't had a single conversation since the day she told him. But every time he was with her, he acted like a guard dog ready to attack anyone who came near her. Her mother was home but now she has to figure out how to have a relationship with her.

"Nattalie... Nattalie?" Zach shook her shoulder trying to snap her from the obvious deep thought she had fallen into.

"Are you okay?"

"No, no I'm not. None of this means anything. If I ran a mile tomorrow, I still can't fix it... any of it."

The disgust in her voice was apparent although Zach was confused about what she meant. "Listen, I'm sure there's quite a story behind all of this. But maybe that's the point of it all." She wiped the few tears that had begun to fill her eyes. "What do you mean?" Zach grabbed a folding chair and sat backward on it next to her.

"Sometimes the pain isn't about you."

"Uhhhh... I'm the one in pain. How isn't it about me?"

"Do you think you're the only one in the world who's experienced pain? Or any of the things you've experienced?"

"I guess not. But so, what? I'm still in pain!"

Zach's smile never left his face. "Wouldn't it be great if you made it through this and then turned around and helped someone else get through their problem?" The thought had never crossed her mind. "You are a strong person Nattalie. I can tell. Don't let this beat you. Your strength and your story maybe the very thing to motivate someone else to keep going." Something about those words lit her up inside and she couldn't help but be motivated by his confidence. □ "So, let's get this work done today girl."

After ending their session Nattalie waited for her Dad and Toni to come pick her up. She knew they would be running late that day. So, she asked to be sat outside so she could watch the fall leaves around the front lawn of the building. They were beautiful and she just wanted a few minutes of quiet. "You gonna cry now?" A voice from behind said. She turned to see the blonde-haired boy standing behind her. "What are you talking about?" Once she saw his face, she was immediately annoyed. He came and sat down next to her.

"I mean you're staring at the trees and bushes as if you're in love with them."

"They happen to be beautiful this time of year and I don't have to explain anything to you. I don't even know you."

He wiped his sweaty hand on his jacket and then reached it out to Nattalie. "I'm Ethan." She sneered at his hand and instead of shaking it she gave a tiny wave in his direction. He laughed and withdrew his hand.

"So, do you have a name?"

"Nattalie."

"Nattalie, that's pretty."

"So, what do you want Ethan?"

"What do you mean?"

"I mean you've been staring at me in my sessions ever since the first day I got here. What's your deal?"

"I'm sorry, I just thought you were pretty and wondered how you ended up here."

"I had an accident. Why are you here?"

"I tried to kill myself. It didn't work."

She was barely able to process what he had just told her before her dad pulled up in his car. Nick hopped out the car. "Hey sweetie I'm sorry you had to wait." Nick looked at Ethan and recognized him from the training room.

"Hi, I'm Nattalie's father. You are?"

"I'm Ethan."

 "Dad he was just waiting for his ride too." Although he never said why he was still there. "Yea, I'm just waiting." Nick nodded his head and continued helping Nattalie in the car. "See ya Nattalie." Ethan said as Nick closed the car door. She didn't respond, just looked at him from the window. As he watched them drive off.

Back at home Toni and Lilian were making dinner. Nattalie was strong enough to walk with a cane at this point. She hobbled into the kitchen and almost fell over at the sight of the two of them together. They actually seemed rather content. "Hey sweetie... Look at you." Lilian almost teared up to see her walking into the kitchen.

"I'm still on a cane mom. Got a long way to go."

"Yes, but you're doing it."

Toni reached into the refrigerator and pulled out a pitcher of Lemonade.

"You feel like a glass?"

"No thanks. No one makes Lemonade like my Aunt Gene."

"Well it's a good thing I stopped by to make it then."

Before she could wonder who's voice it was, Aunt Gene came into the kitchen. "Aunt Gene!" She almost leaped at the sight of her. After a long hug, she poured her a glass of Lemonade.

"When did you get here?"

"Earlier today while you were at therapy. Been having a long chat with your mom and Toni. Now I'm done with them. I want to talk to you."

Both Toni and Lilian knew that was their cue to leave. They sat down at the kitchen table together and just like always talking to Aunt Gene was so easy.

"So, tell me what's going on?"

"Well, I'm in therapy. The brain injury…"

"I know all that dear. I mean tell me about what's going on with you."

"What do you want to know exactly?" Nattalie wasn't sure where to start and certainly didn't want to tell too much.

"For one thing, how are you feeling about losing the baby?"

"I don't feel anything. It was a mistake."

Her eyes were staring at the ground. Aunt Gene used both her hands to lift her head up and looked her in the eyes.

"You're not telling the truth."

"I wanna forget about it and get better. It's better this way."

"That doesn't mean you don't have feelings about it. You keep ignoring them and they'll explode one day in a way that can hurt even more."

☐The memory of the day of her fall played in her mind. It wasn't just her feelings about the baby. It was the way she got pregnant. The death of the sister she'd barely gotten to know. All the way back to her mother leaving and her parent's divorce. Her feelings were too many to sort out. "I can't right now. I just need to get better and be able to get myself from one room to the other like a healthy normal person." She said as she shook her cane in the air. Aunt Gene sipped the last of her Lemonade and reached for Nattalie's hand. "I'll let it go for now dear. But sooner or later you will have to face it head on. I'm here if you need me." They leaned forward and hugged each other tight. As badly as she wanted to tell Aunt Gene everything, she just couldn't bare her shame to anyone else. "By the way dear. Your mom mentioned that your cousin Anderson would be coming to visit soon. With his mom passing away and all, you two probably could help each other." The room was spinning as Aunt Gene's words came crashing over her like black waves. Nattalie felt as if all the blood had drained from her body. Then suddenly, her body went numb and the room went black. Aunt Gene fell to the floor to try and catch her. "Oh my God! Lilian!! Help!" Within seconds the whole family was in the kitchen. Nattalie's Caramel complexion looked almost grey. Nate grabbed a hand towel and ran it under some cold water for her face. Her body was in a sweat. They had moved her to her bed and opened the windows. After several minutes she began to open her eyes. At first her vision was blurred, and she wasn't sure of who was standing over her. As her vision came back into focus, Anderson was staring back at her. "Go away!!!" She screamed as she scrambled to get off the bed. "Nattie stop... we're trying to help you!" Her dad and brother tried to hold her down, but she was stronger than usual. In her panic she got up from the bed forgetting she couldn't walk very well. She collapsed on the floor. "Oh, my goodness!" Lilian cried. "Everybody stay where you!" Nick instructed. "Nate, help me get her up." They both lifted a sobbing Nattalie off the floor. Nate put her in her bed and pulled the curly strands of hair from her sweaty tear stained face. "What happed?" He said looking back at Aunt Gene. "I don't know... I... I was just talking to her and she just fell out!" She said with her hands shaking. "Is he really coming here?" Nattalie asked in a faint voice. "Who sweetie? Is who coming here?" Nick asked as he sat on her bed beside her. She had come to herself again and realized that she couldn't let on that she was afraid for Anderson to come there. Everyone would wonder why. That was a question she wasn't going to answer. "Nothing…I mean... no one dad. I just need some rest. Please just leave me alone a while." Nattalie turned over as if to go to sleep. They all looked at each other so confused as to what just happened. Not wanting to upset her any further, Nick motioned everyone to leave the room as she had asked. "Okay sweetie, we're all here if you need us." He kissed the side of her face and left with the others.

Out in the living room Lilian was pacing the floor.

"What in the hell is going on Nick?"

"I don't know Lily, calm down."

"Calm down? Now she's fainting for no reason? Something is going on here! She's hiding something, I can feel it Nick."

Lilian looked at Aunt Gene who was just as confused as everyone else. "What did you say to her Gene?" Gene was almost frightened at the way Lilian approached her. "Well, I was only encouraging her to deal with her emotions Lily. The girl has been through hell and no one seems to see that she needs more than just physical therapy! Something is wrong Lily, you're right. But only she knows what it is." They all sat in the living room. Worried and feeling helpless. Nate knew that his sister wasn't going to open up to any one of them. If she was going to get better anytime soon, he had to get the whole truth out of her. She opened up to him before. Perhaps she would again.

"Does she have therapy tomorrow dad?"

"No. not till Friday."

"Okay... I want to take her some place after school."

"Ummm son I know you have your license now but…"

"But what dad? She needs to get out of these walls and do something normal. I can handle it. She's my sister."

"Okay but if anything happens you bring her right back home. Got it?"

"Yea, I got it."

The following day after school Nate rushed home to get his homework done so he'd be ready to borrow the car as soon as his dad got home. He sat at the kitchen table struggling to concentrate because of the music coming from Nattalie's bedroom. He was mildly irritated until he realized she was playing Christmas music. Smiling to himself, he went to her bedroom door.

"Hey Nattie, can I come in?"

"Yea, come in."

He stood in the doorway leaning against the frame and smiling.

"Ya know it's only November, right?"

"Since when did we ever wait until December to play Christmas music Nate?" He scratched his head.

"I guess we never did."

"Nope! Mom would start playing Nat King Cole almost right after Halloween it seems."

"To tell you the truth, I'm surprised you're in the holiday spirit at all."

"I'm not actually. I just thought if I played some holiday music, it would help."

"Help what?"

"It doesn't matter. It's not working. It actually made me feel worse."

Nate came in and sat down on the bed next to her while 'Oh little town of Bethlehem' played on her CD player.

"What's worse?"

"It just all seems like such a fairytale. Wise men and bright stars that lead the way. A savior that came to rescue us. After everything that's happened, I can't even believe in a savior. I can't believe in anything."

Nate's heart sank at her words. He hadn't been deeply religious since they were kids, but he still believed there was something beyond himself that could intervene in our lives. "Ya know, dad's been praying a lot since you got hurt. He even read his Bible to you while you were in the coma." She scoffed at his words.

"Whatever makes him feel better. I just want to walk again, without a cane. To go back to school like a normal kid. To get my driver's license like you."

"You will Nattie."

Just then they both heard keys at the front door. Their dad was home.

"Okay, we're going for a drive."

"But where are we going Nate?"

☐ "You'll see."

After about a Fifteen Minute drive in the dark suddenly there was a flood of lights. Nattalie looked up to see an entire street off houses lit up with Christmas lights already. "Remember this Nattie cake?" She smiled as memories began to play in her head.

"Fifth Avenue Nate"

"We haven't been over here since we were like ten years old!"

"Look at all the people that still come here. Oh man... remember mom would bring us here as soon as she heard the lights were up. In fact, she played the Christmas music right after we would come see the lights!"

The memories came rushing in like a fresh breeze.

"Those old cassette tapes of Motown Christmas songs would be playing the whole way home."

Nate looked over at his sister smiling as she recalled such great memories. Memories that somehow got buried under life's trials. He was happy to see her smile and hear her laugh. But her smile gradually began to fade.

"What's wrong Nattie?"

"We used to walk down the block to see the decorations up close. I can't go that far on my cane. What are you smiling at?"

"Just at how smart I am. I put your wheelchair in the trunk. So, you wanna get out?"

She wanted to be upset about having to sit in a wheelchair, but she was too excited about those lights to care.

"Let's do it."

☐ For a little while among those lights and parents who were making the same memories with their kids. Things didn't seem that bad at all.

They returned home and as Nate turned off the car, Nattalie grabbed his arm. "I have to tell you something." Nate turned toward his sister to let her know he was listening.

"I need your help. Anderson is coming back here."

"Wait, what?"

"Just hold on let me finish."

Nate took a deep breath and tried to calm himself down.

"Aunt Gene said he's coming back for a visit. I'm not sure when but I can't tell mom or dad about what happened."

"You have to Nattie! I don't want him anywhere near you!"

"Neither do I, but if I tell it'll destroy what's left of this family! Haven't we been through enough? I've been through enough!"

Nate leaned back in the driver's seat with his hands on top of his head.

"What do you want me to do Nattie?"

"I want you to keep him away from me. Don't leave me alone with him for as long as he's here." Nate's face was turning a deep burgundy.

"You expect me to let my sister's rapist in our house and say nothing? Do nothing!"

"Please…please. I can't bare anything else falling apart. Mom is finally home and actually trying to be a mom. Dad and Toni are doing good together. I'm getting stronger. Our lives could get back to normal soon. Let's just get through this and then forget it all ever happened."

Nate grabbed her hand and squeezed it. "I love you sis. I'll keep quiet only for you. But sooner or later you won't be able to just bury your pain. You gotta deal with it somehow." She didn't want to hear that. It was almost exactly what Aunt Gene said. "Thank you, Nate for tonight. It was fun." He didn't say a word. Just smiled in her direction.

A Way Out

"You got this girl keep going!" Zach cheered Nattalie on as she finished her first unassisted walk since the accident. It was only about ten feet from where Zach was standing to the chair he'd asked her to reach. "WOOO! Yes! I told you that you were ready!" She tried to keep from smiling at such a small victory, but Zach's excitement made it impossible. Finally, after a few moments of playing it cool. She broke and smiled the biggest smile Zach had seen since she came there.

"Wow…"

"What? So, I walked to a chair. Still have a long way to go."

"No, no, it's not just that. You really are a strong girl. I'm proud of you."

In that moment she could feel a connection that she couldn't really explain. When Zach spoke, she didn't feel like he was on the outside looking in. It always felt like he was right there with her. Struggling with her and this day, celebrating with her.

"Let's wrap this up, today shall we?"

"Yes, we shall."

They shared a laugh and began to gather her things so her dad could pick her up. As she headed toward the doors, she suddenly found herself with company.

"Mind if I walk you outside? I see you're getting around that cane a lot better."

"Ethan? Well you don't seem to be having any trouble at all so I'm not sure why you're still here."

"You're not very observant, are you?

"What do you mean?"

"Have you ever seen me use both of my arms at once? See, all the nerve damage trying to kill yourself unsuccessfully can do."

She hadn't really taken notice of the arm he kept cradled to his side or the slight limp he walked with until that moment.

"Look my ride will be here soon and…."

"So, you're scared of me?"

"No. I just don't get why you'd want to brag about trying to kill yourself."

"Oh, come on. Don't tell me you've never thought about it."

"I'm just trying to walk again and get back to my life."

"Ha! And what's that really worth?"

"What is your problem?"

"Hey, I'm just saying that we're all a bunch overgrown pond scum in the grand scheme of things. Evolution's biggest mistake. Why does it matter if we live or die?"

Nattalie wanted to shoot back something uplifting and profound but instead found herself considering his words. At that moment, her dad pulled up and helped her into the car. For the second time, Ethan had left her speechless and burdened with thought.

Nattalie had asked to eat dinner in her room that night. Her thoughts were in too much of a gaggle to try and hold anything resembling a conversation at dinner. Trying to come up with a full proof plan to keep Anderson away from her when he arrived was consuming her. It helped knowing that at least she had Nate there to protect her this time. She'd barely touched her food when someone knocked at her door. "I don't want any dessert guys!" She yelled back. The door popped open and Kelsey poked her head inside. "Well I didn't have any dessert anyway." Kelsey said with a giggle. Nattalie just stared at her. Not really knowing how to react at first. She hadn't seen her since the night she took the pregnancy test at her house.

"Where have you been?"

"I'm so sorry Natt."

"Sorry? Do you even know what I've been through? You show up after all these months! Why are you here?"

"I wanted to come see you. In the hospital when you got home. But my mom wouldn't let me!"

"Your mom? But why?"

"When she heard you were pregnant, she said we couldn't be friends anymore. I couldn't call you or come over or anything!"

Kelsey rushed to Nattalie and hugged her tight. "I'm so sorry. I wanted to see you so bad. I am sorry." After a few seconds of resistance, they were embracing each other. "I missed you too Kelsey." Nattalie pulled away.

"But wait, how did you get over here then?"

"Mom and Dad are out of town visiting my grandparents for two weeks. I'm staying with my Aunt Mary and I've got her car for the evening." She said with vibrato as she dangled a set of car keys from her finger.

"Awesome! Why didn't you go with them?"

"Oh, I had been sick right before the trip and convinced them I wasn't well enough to travel." They both laughed. "So, you gotta fill me in. You haven't been in school, so I need details." Even as awful as the whole story was. It felt good to be able to tell her friend all about it. The coma, Valencia's death, her brain injury, losing the baby. Everything came out in a river of tears.

"I feel sick that I wasn't here with you."

"You're here now. At lease I know you didn't just abandon me."

"Is there anything else you wanna talk about? Am I all caught up?"

"Pretty much. Except this creepy kid that keeps bugging me at my therapy sessions."

"Creepy kid?"

"Yea, Ethan." Nattalie rolled her eyes. "He keeps bragging about how he tried to kill himself."

"Whoa... I'd stay away from that one."

"The weird thing is that he got me thinking."

"What could he possibly make you think about besides running for the hills?"

"Nothing, nothing. Never mind."

"Well since it's nothing why don't we go in the kitchen and get dessert? I saw a pound cake on the table."

☐ Dessert sounded good to Nattalie all of a sudden.

Two days later, Nick was at Nattalie's bedroom door gently knocking. "Nattie, Nattie..." He poked his head inside her door. "Hey, good morning." She rolled over with her curls still in her face. "Hey dad.

What time is it?" She said in a raspy morning voice. "It's almost 9. Toni and I were gonna go to church this morning. I was wanting you and Nate to come along. You feeling up to it?" She was feeling fine until she heard the word 'church.' The whole subject of God made her head feel foggy. Still not understanding why a good God could let her be hurt so badly, she shook her head to decline her dad's offer. "You sure sweetie? We can all go out to breakfast afterwards. We haven't done that in years it seems. Church then family breakfast." Nick chuckled a little to himself. As if remembering the past fondly.

"No thanks dad. Maybe next time. I'd rather rest today."

"Okay Nattie. Maybe next Sunday okay?"

She nodded and smiled. Before her dad could get down the hall good, Nate came into the room. "Hey, so you going?" He flopped on her bed causing her to bounce a little.

"Geeze Nate, don't flop so hard."

"Aw come one. You used to like to bounce on the bed. So, you going to church?"

"Nope. I can't deal with that right now."

"What do you mean? What is there to deal with?" She let out a big sigh and rolled her eyes.

"I can't deal with the God thing right now. I still…… never mind."

"No way. No never mind. Talk to me." She sat herself up in bed and folded her arms.

"I just don't understand how everything got so messed up. How our lives just…. Just. Why did God let this happen to me? And why is He letting Anderson come back here?"

"Look, I know you probably don't want to hear this but you're the reason Anderson is coming back here sis."

"What do you mean?"

"Hey, if you would just tell mom and dad not only would he not be coming here, he'd be in jail!"

"Shhhh...not so loud Nate." She looked at her door cracked open still. Nate got up to close it.

"Listen Nattie, I know you're scared but...."

☐ "No, no. You don't know what this feels like at all. I'm the one who was raped by my cousin. I'm the one who was pregnant with his baby. I'm the one who fell off a roof and was in a coma and my baby died!" She sobbed as she forced her words out through the tears. "I don't even know how to feel about it. I don't know if I should be sad because I lost it or happy because it wasn't right for me to be pregnant by him. I don't even know if it was a boy or girl. Part of me wants to know. The other part just wants to die. An even bigger part wants him to die. Either way I'd free myself from this fear. I'm not certain that anything matters anyway." Do you know what Anderson said to me before the last time he...." She paused not wanting to say it. "He told me, there is no God. Then he showed me just how much God cares about me! So much that he let him hurt me!" Nate had no clue what to do with what he just heard. He was beginning to wonder himself if there was anyone above who cared. All he knew was that he wanted to help her however he could. Whatever the cost, he had to get his sister out of this. "Nattie, I'll see him dead before I see a single hair on your head harmed and I mean it." They looked at each other, speaking with no words. There was nothing Nate wouldn't do for Nattalie.

After wrapping up another physical therapy session, Nattalie hurried as quickly as her cane could assist her toward the door. She had seen Ethan during her session but figured she could get outside and in the car before he could find his way to her. Once she made it outside, she sighed a sigh of relief and sat down to wait on her ride. "Nattalie?" A voice from behind startled her. She looked up to see the receptionist standing there. "I'm sorry to startle you but your father just called. He's running behind from work but on his way." It certainly wasn't what she wanted to hear but she nodded her head at the young woman. "Okay, thanks." She began looking for another possible place to sit in. One where Ethan couldn't find her. "Are you looking for me?" Ethan said limping toward her. If there was ever a time, she wished she could jump up and run, it was then.

"No, I was actually looking for another place to sit for your information."

"Ha! Why? Isn't this where you get picked up at? How would your ride find you if you suddenly moved?" She hated to admit the logic in his thinking. "Dang…. I guess you're right." He sat down next to her. "So, how's it going? You're getting stronger I can see. You don't lean on the cane as much." She shrugged her shoulders. "Yea I guess so." Looking over at his arm left arm that he was holding on his lap. She started feeling a bit sorry for him. She couldn't wrap her mind around how he could attempt suicide and talk so casually about it.

"So… uhh. How are you doing?"

"Ehh. Okay, I guess. I mean I don't think it really matters if I heal or not. My parents are determined to get me better or whatever. At the end of the day we're all headed to an unescapable state of non-being anyway." Nattalie scoffed and rolled her eyes.

"Why do you talk like that? You act like there's absolutely no reason to exist at all!"

"Well, there isn't."

"Yes, there is!"

"Oh yea? Like what? Family? Friends? Or… don't tell me you're one of those God people." She paused. In actuality, she wasn't sure what she was at the moment. "I don't really know right now… just quit with all that crazy talk okay?" She sat back on the bench frustrated. "Okay, I'm sorry kid. Didn't mean to upset you. I just don't see much point to any of it. If we all emerged from the slime and our whole reality was accidental, then what does anything mean? Life is a meaningless cycle and we're all gonna rot in the end." It was like some warped type of preaching the way he spoke about life being meaningless with such conviction.

"How are you so passionate about the subject of meaninglessness?"

"I guess that is weird huh? I just think everyone should wake up. If you wanna stay in this life, then fine. Do what you wanna do and don't let anybody tell you it's wrong. In the end we all rot and that's it."

"What about the stuff that really is wrong?"

"There's no such thing. Wrong? Says who? God? Please, ain't no such thing."

There wasn't anything she could say. After all, she was on a fence with her beliefs. But if there wasn't a God, then what was really the point of doing anything good? She tried to justify it in her mind.

"Well why not just help each other? Shouldn't we want to survive as a species or something?"

"Why?"

"I don't know! I don't know!"

"Look, if you wanna live, then live. If you wanna die, then die. If you wanna kill, then kill. None of it matters in the end."

The fear that spread over her face made her face look gray. "Whoa, Nattalie. Don't get me wrong. I don't wanna hurt anybody." A car pulled up in front of them, but it wasn't her dad's car. "Hey honey!" A voice called from the car window. It was her mom. She hopped out to help her in. "Sorry, but your dad was gonna be even later than he thought. So, I told him I'd get you." Lilian looked at Ethan with curious eyes. And gave a polite smile. "Bye Nattalie." She waved □back at him. For the first time since they met, she didn't want to leave. She was both confused and intrigued.

Ethan's words played in her mind all evening. At the dinner table she sat silent. Rolling a Brussel sprout back and forth with her fork. She loved Brussel sprouts and usually had a second helping. Nathan watched her for about five minutes before he decided to say anything. "Umm how many miles you plan on putting on that sprout?" She looked up confused at his statement. "Huh? What'd you say?" He pointed at her plate. "You've been rolling that Brussel sprout around for a little while now." She looked at her almost completely cold meal and sat her fork down. "I'm sorry. I guess I'm not hungry." Toni got up from her seat and took Nattalie's plate. "Why don't we just wrap this up and maybe you can have it for lunch tomorrow or something." Nattalie was happy that no one made a big deal out of it. She wasn't in the mood for questions. "In fact, how bout I just get dessert out? I picked up a chocolate bunt cake from that little bakery on Rose Lane." She cut a huge slice and put it on a plate for Nattalie. "How 'bout that?" Toni smiled as she sat it in front of her. "Hey! That's so not fair. She gets dessert without eating her dinner." Nate protested. "Jealous much?" Nattalie said as she stuck her tongue out at him. Nick, who had been quiet most of the evening himself, laughed almost choking on his food.

"Looks like a little bit of jealousy to me son."

"Yea, whatever dad."

Nick shook his head looking at his daughter, who at that moment looked about five years old as she ate big forks full of the cake. Making exaggerated eating noises at her brother. "Okay, you two. How about we talk about Christmas? I was thinking we could have a Christmas party this year." Nate and Nattalie looked at each other, then looked back at their dad. "Well we haven't had one of those since we were little." Nate said with a chuckle. "I know! Look, it's been a rough crazy year for all of us. But despite all that's gone on, God has been good and I'm grateful. So, I don't want to mope around over the holidays, wishing things had been better or whatever. I have both my kids alive and with me when I could just have one." Then he looked at Nattalie. "I know it's been a long hard road and you're still trying to navigate it sweetheart, but I want to celebrate how far you've come. I want you to smile and laugh and remember that there is still joy to be found in life." His eyes filled with tears. Although his speech didn't launch her back into full blown faith. She looked into his eyes and in that moment, Ethan's voice disappeared. "Okay daddy. A party sounds good. Let's do it." He got up and kissed her hard on her cheek. "Ewww, dad stop." Nate got up to get himself some cake. "Well we've only got a few weeks to plan so we'd better get a guest list together." Toni grabbed a note pad and pen then sat back at the table. "Okay, start giving me names. I'll call Lilian and get names from her too." It was still weird to Nate and Nattalie how friendly the two of them were now. "I know Anderson will be there." Toni said as she wrote. Nattalie's stomach turned. She'd almost forgotten he was supposed to be coming back in town. But she kept quiet while they continued their planning. Her mind once again began replaying Ethan's words. She considered the possibility that he was right. Then her mind went to a place it had never been before and she became afraid of herself.

The night was clear, and it seemed like every star in the universe was out. It was quiet. But almost too quiet. Nattalie was looking for a distraction from her unsettling thoughts. The patio door slid open and Nate walked out. He wrapped an old quilt around her shoulders.

"Hey, thanks. I was getting cold." He sat down on the chase next to her.

"I figured. I wasn't sure why you wanted to sit out here in the cold in the first place."

"It's not that bad. Remember Minnesota that winter? Now that was cold." She looked off into the trees for a moment. "Now the cold is coming here." She tightened the quilt around her. "Sis, did he hurt you on that trip?" Flipping her curls out of her face she laughed.

"It doesn't matter. He's not going to hurt me again."

"No, he's not. I'll make sure of that."

"You don't understand. He is never going to hurt me again." Nate was confused. Until he looked in her eyes and saw her mind. "What are you going to do Nattalie?" Tears rolled down her cheeks. "I'm going to give myself the best Christmas present ever. I'm making a way out of this fear. If I'm going to live, then he has to die." The shock of her words paralyzed him. Still somehow, he didn't resist the idea. He had thought about killing Anderson many times since she confessed what he had done to her. Between the guilt of not protecting her and the pain of watching her suffer. Revenge seemed more a delicious idea than ever. He sat back and looked up at the stars.

"There are a lot of stars out tonight huh?"

□ "Yup, there sure are. But they're just an accident of nature. They don't mean anything. It's all meaningless."

Party Planning

Lights, bows and festive banners were sprawled out over the family room floor. Lilian was busy helping Toni mail out the last of the invitations. She and Toni had been getting along so well that she hadn't thought about the fact that most of the guest list were old friends that she and Nick had before their divorce. The thought made her feel uncomfortable. "You okay Lily?" Toni asked after noticing her sudden sad expression. "Ummm, yea. Well…" Lilian struggled to put her thoughts into words. Finally, she turned toward Toni and grabbed both her hands. "Listen, I'm happy to help you guys get this party together. But I don't think I should be there." Toni was confused by her words.

"What are you talking about? You know you're invited."

"Yes, but these guests were friends of mine and Nick while we were married. I behaved so badly for so long during our marriage and everyone knows it. It would be too weird, and I'd be too embarrassed to face everyone."

"Won't you at least come for the kids? I know they want you there." Lilian sighed with her face toward the floor.

"Maybe just for a little while. I can't promise all night."

☐ "If you feel uncomfortable at any point, then you can go. But I hope you stay. Besides, if you knew half of what these other married couples went through behind closed doors. You'd think your divorce was a fairy tale in comparison." They both laughed together. "Toni you are something else. I don't know why you've always been so kind to me. Even when I was mean to you." Toni smiled and then threw a bow at her. "There! Now we're even." She laughed. "Now let's separate these colors and figure out how we can make some magic in this house."

While the two of them buried themselves in holiday cheer. Nathan helped Nattalie navigate through a kitchen piled with plastic bins and totes filled with old Christmas decorations. "Mom!" He yelled out. "Can you guys find somewhere else to put this stuff for now!" Lilian came into the kitchen to find Nate guide his sister through the narrow space they had left for walking through the kitchen. "Oh, I'm sorry honey. Here I'll move this stuff right now." She clambered trying to quickly make a wider space. "It's okay mom, chill. I got this." Nattalie said, seeing how mildly panicked her mom was. That morning was going pretty good for her physically. She wasn't leaning on her cane as much as she had been, and her strides seemed longer.

"Where are you two headed to anyway?"

"To the library mom." Nattalie said with a slight irritability in her voice. "Yea... I need to look up some stuff for an essay. Thought I'd get Nattie out of the house." Nate explained, trying to cover for Nattalie's attitude. Lilian looked at them both and it was apparent that they were avoiding eye contact.

"Is everything okay?"

"Yes!" They both exclaimed at once. She wasn't convinced but decided to let it go for now.

"Okay well be careful and don't keep your sister out too late Nate."

☐ "Mom, I'm fine. Keeping me out late isn't going to make anything worse." Nattalie jerked her arm away from Nate who had been holding on to her. Then she limped toward the front door. Nate was about to walk after her when Lilian grabbed his arm. "Anything I need to know son?" He wanted to tell her, but it was so crazy that she might not even take him seriously if he did. He barely believed what they were plotting to do himself. "No mom. There's nothing you should know." With that he hurried out to help Nattalie into the car.

After arriving at the library, they didn't quite know where to start. "What exactly are we looking for Nattie?" Nate asked in a loud whisper.

"We need to find something on poisons and something on serial killers."

"Why serial killers? We're not going on a killing spree."

"Maybe and maybe not. Doesn't really matter."

"Have you gone insane Nattie?"

"SHHHH. I'm not crazy. Just find the books please."

"I don't even know where to start." Nattalie pointed to a counter with an elderly lady standing behind it.

"Go ask her where to look."

"She'll be suspicious."

"No, she won't. Just tell her it's for a school project."

Nate could barely keep his balance as he nervously approached the counter. He wiped his sweaty palms against his pants and cleared his throat before attempting to get the lady's attention. "Excuse me ma'am." The lady looked up at him with a smile.

"How can I help you?"

"I was looking for a book on common poisons and also for a book on serial killers."

His voice was high and cracked. While he cleared his throat, the ladies smile quickly disappeared. "It's for a school assignment." He gave an awkward smile to neutralize the bewildered look on her face. She went to her computer and began to type. After a couple of minutes, she wrote on an index card and gave it Nate. "This is the section you can find books on poisons and this is the section you'll find the killers." She said pointing at her notes. "Thank you, ma'am." He helped Nattalie find a seat while he searched for the right books.

Nate kept looking over his shoulder as he searched the shelves. He began to worry that someone he knew would show up and be curious about why he was looking up poisons. He was ready to give up after just a few minutes. He needed an excuse to get out of this. Telling Nattalie that he wasn't going through with it wasn't an option. Letting her down again was more than he could handle. Still he couldn't completely embrace what they were doing. His palms started to sweat again, and he wanted to run. "Can I help you with something?" A voice startled him from behind. "I'm so sorry to startle you but you looked like you needed help." Nate turned to see a pretty young woman with a library uniform shirt on. "uhhh…pa…poisons. I need a book on poisons." The young woman stooped down to the bottom shelf and pulled out a green book with a frog on the front of it. "Ah here we go. Exotic and Common poison." She handed the book to him with a smile. "Is that all you need?" She was so pretty and bubbly Nate almost forgot what he needed the book for. "Oh... uh. Killers. I need a book on serial killers." The young lady gave a puzzled look.

"Research paper or something?"

"Uh yea. That's exactly it."

"Sure, follow me."

He followed her to another section and was almost lost in how alive she seemed. Her smile and her lighthearted demeanor made him long for the days before their world was turned upside down. Then he remembered why they were there and why he couldn't back down. "Okay here we are. Famous serial killers." She handed him a book with pictures of the most recognizable killers on the planet on the cover. "Is that all?" He clutched both books to himself.

"Yes, that's all. You've helped a lot. Thank you."

"You're welcome."

Nate watched her as she walked away. Thinking it would be ashamed if she knew exactly what she had helped him do. He returned to where Nattalie was sitting.

"Well dang, it took you long enough Nate."

"Chill, okay. I got 'em." They both were on edge. Nattalie snatched the serial killer book from the table. "I'll start reading about how these guys did it. You find out what's the easiest poison to get. Skip the exotic stuff." They both started thumbing through the contents. It was only a matter of minutes before Nate found something useful. "Hey, check this out." Nattalie scooted closer to see what he was pointing at. "It's called strychnine. It's primarily used as a pesticide to kill rats. In humans it can cause severe painful muscles spasms. Eventually the muscles tire and the person stops breathing." They looked at each other nervously.

"This is it Nate."

"It is?"

"Yes. There's rat poison in the garage. I've seen it."

"No, no. Dad doesn't have that anymore."

"You're lying Nate."

"I'm not. It got knocked over the last time we were reorganizing his tool shelf."

"Fine, we'll just have to find something else. ☐Look, look. How 'bout this? Arsenic."

"Arsenic?"

"Yea. This says it's almost the perfect murder weapon. In large doses it can kill a person within 24hrs, and the symptoms often get mistaken for other illnesses." She slammed the book shut. "This is it and I know where we can get it." She stared off into space as she spoke.

"Where are we gonna find arsenic?"

"At school."

"What?!" He shrieked.

"SHHHH. Yes, at the school. Chemistry class. There's a whole bottle of it in Mr. Feinstein's class. You could get it."

"So now I have to be a thief too?"

"What does it matter?"

"What does it matter? It's wrong that's what matters Nattalie?"

"Listen don't you back out on me now when I need you."

"I don't wanna back out on you sis but I'm having second thoughts. I just wish there was a better way for you to heal."

"I don't want to heal. I want revenge. I want to take everything from him like he's taken everything from me. Now are you with me?" Nate wanted to scream 'NO' as loud as he could. But looking into her tear-filled eyes all he could manage to do was nod his head.

"Good. You can get it from class, but you'll have to do it the last day before winter break. That way no one will have time to notice it's gone. Mr. Feinstein shows movies on the last day. No one will notice anything is missing."

She opened the serial killer book and pointed to a picture. "You see this guy here? All of his wives were heavy drinkers and when he got tired of it, he poisoned their dinner wine. A little bit at a time so it looked like they were just ill. Eventually they all died." Nate leaned closer to her. "Anderson likes to drink." Her eyes narrowed and she gave him a sinister smile. "Exactly. Let's make it his last drink."

The next few weeks were a whirl wind of preparations for the party. After Lilian and Toni hashed out the final guest list, there were eighty-five invitations sent out. The RSVP responses were coming in fast too. Nattalie helped Toni make the shopping list for the menu. "So, what did you and dad do? Rent new friends?" Toni giggled at her question.

"Now why would you say that?"

"I'm just trying to figure out where all these people are coming from." Toni peeked at Nattalie's list to see if there was anything she wanted to add. "Well some are my friends and family as well." It never dawned on Nattalie that they had never met any of Toni's family before. She spent so much time at their house, she really had become part of the family. "Toni, do you love my dad?" She sat down the pen she'd been writing with and looked Nattalie in the eye.

"Yes, I love him very much."

"I guess I already knew that. I just…."

"What is it?" Nattalie sat up straight and blew a hard breath. "It's just been weird. I mean my mom coming home after my accident was a shock. She's really been trying to be here for me ya know? But you've been here for so long now. I guess I'm feeling like I have to choose or something. Which is weird because I didn't really want you here in the beginning. I guess I got use to you and I like how you treat my dad." Toni shook her head and sat next to her. "I love your father and I love you and Nate. But I'm not your mother and I'd never want you to feel like you had to choose." Nattalie sighed. "If you feel like you want to get closer to your mom then do that. I can just be a good friend." Toni brushed back the curls that laid over her forehead and gave her a hug. "Thank you, Toni. I guess I do want to get closer to my mom and I will eventually." Toni looked confused. "Why not right now? She'll be by tomorrow I think." Nattalie turned her head to stare out the kitchen window where the garage roof was in plain sight. "There's something I have to do first."

While the two of them continued their list, there was a knock at the door. Before Toni could get up to answer it, Nate came rushing into the living room. He flung open the door to see Kelsey standing there. "Oh, it's just you." He said with disappointment in his voice.

"Well excuse me. Sorry I'm not anyone more interesting."

"Whatever Kelsey. I thought you were my pizza. Anyway, Nattalie's in the kitchen." Kelsey bounced her way to the kitchen. "Hey, hey, everybody!" She flung her arms around Nattalie almost knocking her off the stool she sat on.

"Hey Kelsey, I'm already broken enough don't cha think?"

"Ummmm, I think I can cause a lil' more damage." Toni grabbed Nattalie's note pad.

"If you're done with this, I'll be going to the store this weekend to start getting the stuff that we can store till the party."

"Yea I'm done."

"Okay well then I will see you tomorrow. Bye Kelsey, nice to see you."

"By Ms. Toni." Kelsey reached inside her purse and pulled out a little bag and sat it in front of Nattalie.

"What's this?"

"Just look and see." Nattalie opened the bag and pulled out a pair of heart shaped hoop earrings.

"Oh, these are so cute! Thank you!"

"I thought you'd like them. Put 'em on! Here use my compact so you can see how they look." She put the earrings on and held the compact mirror up to see how they looked. She stared at her reflection for a few moments. It was like looking at a stranger. She stared, trying to remember the last time she put earrings on. Or the last time she took a long hard look at herself in the mirror. She'd been avoiding mirrors up until that point. That face that she thought would never clear of acne. Those eyes that Anderson thought were so beautiful. Nothing in that mirror felt like it belonged to her. Just pieces of a person who was slowly disappearing and she was desperate to get back.

"What's wrong Nattie? I thought you liked them."

"Oh, I do. I do. I just got lost in a thought. Thank you again."

"How about we plan a mall date as soon as you're well?"

"You sure your mom will let you? I'm surprised you're here."

"I'm driving now, and she can't control who I meet at the mall."

Nattalie took the earrings off and placed them back in the bag.

"Listen, things may get a little more complicated around here soon. Maybe it's best that we keep our distance for a while."

"I don't understand. Why?"

"Just trust me! I need you to stay away for just a little while. I can't tell you why." Kelsey's eyes filled with tears as she grabbed her purse and headed out of the kitchen. She stopped suddenly and turned to Nattalie. "I don't know what's going on, but I want my friend back!" Nattalie's lips quivered. "I'm trying to get her back." Kelsey shook her head and left.

On the way to physical therapy with her mom the next day, Nattalie could barely stay still in her seat. She squirmed and even when she managed to keep herself somewhat still, she rubbed her palms together until they were red. "Are you okay?" Her mother asked, noticing how unsettled she seemed. "Yea, I'm just ready to get this session over with. I'm tired of coming here." But that wasn't the whole truth. Although she was tired of physical therapy. She was really anxious about seeing Ethan again. At this point she had given up on God and Ethan's words were all that made since to her anymore. If he really believed all that he had said before, then maybe he'd even be willing to help her and Nate. They finally pulled up in front of the building. A nurse came out to help her out of the car. "I can stay for a little while if you want me to sweetie." Lilian called out from the car window. "No mom. Just pick me up afterwards. I'm fine." She walked into the lobby expecting to see Zach waiting on her. But he wasn't there. "Where is Zach?" She asked the nurse who had assisted her into the lobby. "He's waiting on you in the training room. He asked that you come unassisted today. Think you can handle it?" Truth is that she had been getting around pretty good on her own. Although she was still using the cane, her legs were much stronger than in the beginning. Taking steps wasn't as much of a mental task as it had been. So, she was relieved that Zach felt confident enough in her progress to insist that she make the walk to the training room on her own. "I got it." She said to the nurse with certainty in her voice. Down the hall she went until she got to the training room where Zach was waiting. "There she is!" He shouted out with a smile.

"How are you feeling?"

"I'm pretty good Zach." He nodded his head and reached his hand out to her. "Nattalie I want you to hand me your cane and walk straight down the middle of this room until you reach that wall." She looked at the hard wood floor, then back at Zach. "Don't worry about falling. I'm here and I won't let you get hurt." She stood up straight and steadied herself. Then handed Zach her cane. Looking down at her feet, her first step was wobbly and the second felt as if she might fall. She looked to see if Zach had made a move to break her possible fall, but he hadn't. "You got this Nattalie. Straighten up and take your time. Quit looking down, you're stronger than you think." Then she looked straight ahead and began to take more steps. Halfway across the room, she wasn't wobbling just walking carefully. Finally, just a few feet away from the wall, she took two big strides then rested against the wall. "YEAH!! That's what I'm talking about!" Zach shouted as he applauded her. Suddenly the other patients in the room were applauding her too. Tears filled her eyes as she realized that she was really going to walk normally again. But as she looked around the room at all the patients cheering for her, she noticed that Ethan wasn't there. When the session was over Zach walked with Nattalie back to the lobby. "I'm so proud of you. Keep practicing at home without the cane. I don't expect to be seeing you very much longer." They both stopped at the glass sliding doors.

"Can I ask you something Zach?"

"Sure, what's up?"

"A while back ago you said that my story might help someone else."

"Yes, that's right."

"I guess I'm wondering how you know that." He laughed a little.

"Well, when I was eighteen, I was in a bad car accident. It was my first year in college and I made the decision to get in the car with some friends who had been drinking. We were driving down a narrow back road a few miles from a truck rest stop. My friend who was driving went into the opposite lane and we crashed head on into a semi-truck."

"Oh my God! How are you even alive?"

He hung his head and for the first time she saw him look sad. "I was the only one who survived. But I was hospitalized for months and had to learn how to walk again." A light came on for her at that moment.

"That's why you became a physical therapist?"

"Yup! Sure is. My physical therapist was the reason I even wanted to try and get my life back. I had given up before I met her. My friends were dead, and it seemed so unfair for me to still be alive. But she told me something that stuck with me."

"What did she tell you?"

"She told me that gifts aren't always fair or deserved. I'd been given a gift and I could honor my friends best by not wasting it. So now I try to do for others what she did for me."

Now she was confused. Although she was moved by his story. It was in direct conflict with what Ethan had been talking about and what she had been thinking. Either life was random and meaningless, or it wasn't. Zach certainly seemed to believe his life had meaning, even after such a tragedy. The sudden war of thoughts in her head made her irritable. "Thanks Zach. You've been great but I just don't see how my issues can do anyone else any good." Her mothers' car pulled up in front of the door. As she was about to walk out, she remembered Ethan. "Oh, wait Zach!" She called out before he disappeared around the corner. "Do you happen to know if that blond kid, Ethan, if he still comes to sessions?" Zach walked back over to her with a saddened look on his face. This was the second sad look she'd seen from him in one day. Which instantly worried her. "I'm sorry Nattalie but he's dead. Word is he committed suicide."

The next few weeks were a blur of tinsel, bows, menus, and Christmas music. It was early the Monday morning before the party and Nattalie was in the kitchen making scrambled eggs and bacon without her cane. It was the first time she had made herself a meal since her accident. When no one was around she would practice walking without her cane. Up and down the hall with Ethan's words on repeat in her mind. Every time she took a step, she wondered what it was for. She wanted to get her life back but couldn't justify why she felt it was so important. "Why not just kill myself?" She thought out loud many times. "Why am I trying to walk again when I'm just gonna rot one day anyway? Why not just get it over with now like Ethan?" These thoughts were present every day but still she kept trying to walk. Because she finally settled on a reason to live, at least for the moment. Revenge. She wouldn't live in a world where Anderson was free to do as he pleased. She worked hard to be able to stand on her own. So as god of her own world, she could dispense justice as she saw fit.

Alarm clocks started going off in the bedrooms. She had been up way before anyone else. Nick immediately smelled the bacon frying when he opened his eyes. At first, he thought Toni had come over and was making breakfast. Then he realized that she never came over that early. He got up to see what was going on. Nate entered the hall at the same time.

"Hey dad, is Toni here?"

"I don't think so."

They both walked into the kitchen to see Nattalie standing on her own and making herself a plate. "Good morning. I left some bacon for you guys. Wasn't sure if you wanted eggs." Tears rolled down Nick's face. He went to his daughter and hugged her tight. "Dad you're gonna cut off my circulation." She laughed. "How? When? I mean you're …. You're." He was lost for words, so he just held her and whispered. "Thank you, God, thank you God." Over and over again. Nate stood back trying to control his emotions. For that moment she looked like the sister he knew before. His thoughts became optimistic that maybe just maybe she had dropped this crazy plan to kill Anderson. He could only hope that her heart had healed along with her legs. It was five days before the party and Anderson would be in town soon. If she hadn't changed her mind he wouldn't be leaving.

Dead Man at the Door

   Seven o'clock on Friday morning and Nattalie was gently tapping on Nate's bedroom door.

"Are you up Nate?"

"Yea but why are you up?"

"Can I come in?"

"Yea." Nate threw on a shirt as she entered the room.

"So, you know what you have to do today?"

"I know."

   He sat on the edge of his bed staring at the floor. Hoping that he'd wake up from this nightmare at any moment. But when he raised his head nothing had changed. His sister glared at him as if to let him know she wasn't backing down.

"Get as much of it as you can."

"There won't be a ton of it sis. Just enough for class experiments."

"Whatever they have I want it!"

"Lower your voice, geez."

"I'm sorry. Look just get it for me. It'll all be over before ya know it." She patted him on his shoulder and began to walk out.

"Nattie. Are we really doing this?"

   For a moment she paused but never turned around to answer him. She simply walked out and softly shut the door behind her. Nate sat on the edge of his bed sobbing. He didn't know the girl who he had just been talking to. It felt like his 'Nattie Cake' was dead. So, who was he without his twin? Just a henchman for this new version of Nattalie who had him bound by guilt.

Time moved faster than usual for Nate that day at school. Chemistry was his last class of the day and with every bell that rang from class to class he felt a stabbing sensation in his stomach. Finally, he was in the last class period of the day. Walking into the class he noticed Mr. Feinstein's keys to the supply cabinets hung up on the wall by his desk. He walked close to the wall so he could slip them off the hook and then hurried to his seat.

"Okay guys. I don't know about you, but my brain is already on Christmas break. So, you're gonna watch one of my favorite movies while I grade your final exams."

Just as he was about to cut the lights off, Kelsey walked into the room. Obviously not caring about being late, she even stopped to chat with a friend of hers before she went to her seat.

"Ms. Borders, I know it's the day before break but could you please find your seat so we can get on with the movie?"

"Sorry Mr. Feinstein."

Her seat assignment was right behind Nate. Mr. Feinstein was a fan of seating students in alphabetical order. But Nathan Blythe hadn't thought of Kelsey Borders as anything more than his sister's friend until now. As soon as the lights went out, he turned around to whisper to Kelsey.

"Hey." Nate whispered.

"Hey yourself."

"I uhhhh. I need your help Kelsey."

"My help? Since when do you need my help?"

"Since now."

"This ought to be good. What is it?"

"Look it's important. It's... it's for Nattalie"

"Well what is it?" Kelsey had been worried about her ever since their last meeting.

"I need to get something out of the cabinet in the back but I gotta get Feinstein to leave the room."

"Okay. What am I supposed to do?"

"See that huge slushy on his desk?"

"Yea."

"Go ask him for a hall pass and then accidentally knock it over."

"How is that gonna get him out the room?"

"He'll have to go down the hall for a mop. Then I can grab what I need before he gets back."

"What is it you need so bad?"

"Don't worry about it. It's for Nattalie. Will you help me please?"

"Okay I'll help you."

Kelsey reluctantly made her way to Mr. Feinstein's desk. While she was talking to him, Nate waited anxiously for that slushy to hit the floor. He watched as she knocked it over onto his lap.

"Oh, I'm so sorry, Mr. Feinstein! It was an accident!" The class laughed as he stood up covered in red slushy.

"Now that's enough class! Ms. Borders take your hall pass and go. Class I'll be back as soon as I can find something to clean this mess up with." They both walked out, and Nate slipped to the back of the class in the dark to the supply cabinet. He nervously fumbled through glass jars and containers with a pocket flashlight. Until he saw a clear vile marked "Arsenic Trioxide." He slipped it into his pocket and quickly locked it back. When he sat back down his chest was drenched in sweat. He put his head down on the desk and tried to calm himself down. A hand touched his back and he almost leaped out of his seat.

"Whoa. It's just me Nate. Did you get it?"

"Kelsey. Yea, yea, I got it."

"You don't look so good."

"I don't feel so good either."

"What's wrong?"

"Meet me in the courtyard after school. Please." She had never seen him so unhinged and the look of desperation and fear on his face sent a shiver down her spine.

"Okay I'll meet you."

The bell rang and Nate bolted out of the classroom. He ran out into the courtyard where he found himself vomiting into a bush. Stooped over with his hands on his knees he tried to catch his breath. Again, a hand touched him on the back and he almost ran again.

"Sheesh Nate! What's wrong with you? Are you sick?" He stood up and grabbed her hand.

"Come this way."

"Slow down. Where are we going?" He pulled her into the shade of tree with a little bench underneath and sat down.

"Are you going to tell me now what's going on? What did you need from that cabinet?"

He hung his head low. "It was for Nattalie."

"What was for Nattalie?"

"The Arsenic." His voice quivered.

"Arsenic? But you said it was for Nattalie?" She stood up from the bench.

"No please. You don't understand. Please sit down." She sat back down slowly.

"It is for Nattalie. She asked me to get it for her."

"But why would she need that?"

He hung his head low again. "She's going to kill Anderson." He looked up to see Kelsey's reaction. She looked like a dear in head lights. Frozen. It took her a minute to process what she had just heard.

"She can't be serious."

"I just stole arsenic from my chemistry class. Do you think this is a joke?"

"Wait a minute. That means I helped you do it. I'm a part of this now! How could you?"

"I was desperate! I have to help her."

"Why, why do you have to help her?"

"Because it's all my fault!" Tears came rushing down his face as he began to sob.

"What's your fault?"

"I saw it. I saw the way he looked her when we were in Minnesota☐. I knew something wasn't right with him. I should've stayed and protected her. Everything she's been through is because I left her alone." She put her arms around him and they both shed tears.

"Listen to me Nate. It's not your fault. Anderson is sick and he needs help but first we need to help Nattalie for real. She can't do this."

"But what do I do? I can't let her down again. I want justice but I don't want to be a murderer." He buried his head in his lap. "Dear God please get me out of this."

"When is she gonna do it?"

"Tomorrow night at the Christmas party."

"Maybe I can come and distract her."

"No! She'll know I told you. Look I'm sorry I got you mixed up in this, but I can't let you come to the party."

"So, you use me to get what you need and now you don't want me mixed up in it? Yea no way."

"You have to stay away."

"If you wanted me to stay away then why did you even tell me?" He paused for moment but couldn't give her an answer.

"I'm sorry I said anything Kelsey. It was a mistake. Just go home." He got up from the bench and started to walk away. "Nate! I love her too! Let me help you!" She called out to him, but he kept walking. He wanted her help but thought that it wouldn't be fair to involve her any further.

"Hurry up you guys! I have to pick the ham up in twenty minutes!" Nick yelled from the living room jingling his keys in his hand. Nate came running into the living room. "Nattalie said she'd wait here since we're in a rush. She's still not moving very fast." Nick opened the door and tossed the keys to Nate. "You can drive me today. The way you drive we'll be there in ten minutes." They both laughed walked out the door. No sooner than they were out of the driveway the phone rang. It rang a few times before Nattalie could get to the phone.

"Hello."

"Hey sweetie it's mom."

"Oh, hey mom. What's up? You coming by today?"

"I'll be over later. I just wanted to let your dad know that I'm picking Anderson up from the airport in about an hour."

"Ummm, are you c-coming here right after?"

"No, no, I'm going to get him settled in his hotel room. You probably won't see him until the party tomorrow night. We've all got so much to do between now and then."

"Oh … well uhh. Why isn't he staying here at the house again?"

"Well normally he would but we figured that it would be more comfortable for him to stay in a hotel rather than have to figure out sleeping arrangements and all that."

"But we've got room here mom. You know that."

"Honey it's no big deal. You'll get to see him. Now just give your dad the message and I'll see you later on."

"Sigh. okay see you later. Bye."

Anderson not staying with them definitely made it harder to kill him. Her heart was pounding, and she felt dizzy. But then she had a thought. Maybe it was better that he stayed in a hotel. If she could slip the arsenic in a drink and get him to take it back to the hotel with him. That would be much better than him dying in the house. There was a case of champagne in the dining room for the party. She grabbed a bottle and hid it in her room under the bed. The same bed where Anderson had raped her would conceal her ticket to freedom. The pain of that night surged through her body like a heat wave. For a moment it was happening all over again. Any bit of remorse she had left for what she was planning to do was gone. She got up to make a phone call.

☐ "Hey Toni. It's Nattalie. I want a new dress for the party. Think you could take me to the mall today?"

"I'm pretty sure I can squeeze that in. You'll have to shop quick though. I've gotta pick up the desserts for the party by four o'clock."

"Oh, I won't take long. I just feel like wearing something nice. Tomorrow is a big night."

That night Nattalie had a strange dream. She was walking through a field of tall grass with Ethan. At first, she was walking willingly with him. Then suddenly he began to drag her by her arm. She screamed for him to let her go but he kept pulling her toward a big river with black waves that crashed against the rocks. "Stop it Ethan! Let me go!" She screamed but he kept pulling her closer and closer to the river. Just when they were at the river's edge, she heard a voice call her name in the dark. When she looked over her shoulder, she saw Valencia standing there reaching for her. "Nattalie fight harder!"

Nattalie called back to her. "I can't Valencia! He's too strong!"

"Don't let him pull you in the river! You can't swim! Fight Nattalie! It's not too late!"

At that moment Valencia picked something up off the ground and cradled it in her arms. It was a moment before Nattalie realized that it was a baby.

"It's a boy Nattalie! Fight for him!"

"I'm not strong enough Valencia!" She wailed and sobbed as she fought to free herself from his grip. Finally, she grew tired of resisting him and let him throw her into the black river. Her body hit the cold water and she woke up. Sweating and panting heavily with tears rolling down her cheeks. She took a minute to steady herself before getting out of bed. As her feet hit the floor, she felt something cold touch them. The champagne bottle she hid there had rolled from the spot she put it in. She picked it up and could hear Valencia's voice from the dream saying, "Fight!" Then she began wondering about the baby in the dream. Somehow, she knew it was the baby she'd lost. She wanted to fight but the journey had been long and hard enough. It was time to end it.

By that next evening, the house looked more beautiful than any of them had seen it in years. The Temptations were singing Christmas songs on the stereo. Nick had outdone himself with the Christmas lights both outside and inside the house. The air was filled with the smell of pies and cinnamon. Everyone had been so cheerful all day and right on time the first guest began to arrive. "Hey uncle Johnny!" Nate greeted an older gray-haired man with a cane in his hand and cigar in his mouth.

"Hey, hey, nephew! Last time I saw you, you were knee high to a duck." He laughed at his own comment. Wheezing in between breaths.

"It hasn't been that long Uncle Johnny. Let me take your hat and coat." Nate showed his uncle to the food and went to greet the other guest that were arriving. Only thirty minutes in and the house was full. Nick and Nate had been so busy talking and catching up with family they hadn't noticed Nattalie wasn't in the room. When Nick noticed he sent Nate to go check on her. Nate tapped on her bedroom door.

"Hey Nattie. You coming out soon?"

"Yea in just a minute."

Standing in from of a full-length mirror in a short black evening dress, Nattalie turned her body side to side. It had been months since she'd dressed up in anything other than sweatpants and leggings.

"Can I come in?" Nate tapped the door again and cracked it open.

"Sure, come on. I'm ready."

Nate took a moment to admire his beautiful twin sister. "You look great sis."

"Yea, ya think? I still can't wear heels yet." She looked down at the ballet flats she was wearing.

"You don't need em. Now you ready? The family can't wait to see you."

"Wait. Is uhhh, Anderson here yet?" She shut her door behind Nate.

"I haven't seen him yet." He put his hands on his sister's shoulders. "Are you sure you wanna do this sis? I mean it's going to be a great night. We haven't had this much family around since we were little. Dad is happy and for the first time in a long time I'm not afraid that mom is gonna ruin it all." They both laughed.

"I know but when will we have another opportunity like this?"

"But Nattie...."

"No buts Nate. You said you'd help me. He deserves to die for what he did to me."

"Aren't you afraid though? Just a little bit?"

"Afraid of what?"

"God."

She turned and looked at herself in the mirror one more time and admired her frame. "I am god." She said in a confident voice.

Nate had no response. His faith was shaky now a days but never had he dared make such a boast. Nattalie bent down to grab the champagne bottle from underneath her bed. She sat it on her nightstand.

"This is what we're gonna do. We'll wait until the party is almost over and people start leaving. When it looks like Anderson is ready to go, you'll offer this last bottle of champagne for him to take back to his hotel room."

"Okay, but how will you get the poison inside? It's an unopened bottle."

"I'll open it and you can just tell him that it's a bottle we started but we don't want to waste it."

"I guess that could work."

"You've seen how he drinks. He won't care. It'll work."

Nate nodded his head and grabbed the bottle from the nightstand. "Let's just do it now."

"Wait no not now! You want him to die in front of everybody?"

"I mean let's put the poison in the bottle now and then shove the cork back in. That way we won't have to sneak and do it later."

Nattalie's heart was beating so fast she had to catch her breath.

"What's wrong Nattie? You nervous?"

"Maybe a little bit. But I'll be fine. It's the only way."

As angry as Nate was, he didn't believe that. There had to be another way for his sister to heal but he didn't know what he could say that she would listen to. So, he opened the bottle and slowly poured the arsenic inside until they both saw the bottle was empty. After shoving the cork back inside the bottle and placing it on the nightstand, they took each other by the hand and walked out to join the party.

The music was cheerful and there were smiles and laughs everywhere they looked. Aunt Gene was the first to see the twins walk into the room. Her eyes filled with tears to see Nattalie walking on her own. She rushed to hug them both. "Mwen renmen ou." She said as she grabbed them both. Neither of them had to ask their dad what she said. They knew those words meant 'I love you.' Those three words were the most recognizable Creole words they knew. They heard them a lot between their dad and Aunt Gene growing up.

"We love you too Aunt Gene." Nattalie said as she fought back tears. More and more family came to hug and greet them. Some already a little tipsy and others who were shocked at how much they'd grown up since seeing them last. Mostly everyone was glad to see Nattalie walking again.

After a lot of tears and hugs the Christmas music suddenly stopped. The sound of Al Green's 'Love and Happiness' was now filling the room. Courtesy of Uncle Johnny who was now playing DJ. They all began to dance and sing. Even their dad and Toni were showing off some moves. Once the soul train line commenced even Nattalie had to join in. Nate danced a slow two step with her down the line. Followed by Aunt Gene and Uncle Joe with some ballroom spins. It was the most fun they'd had in a long time. Feeling thirsty, Nattalie went into the kitchen to get some water. When she came back into the living room, she saw the front door opening. Figuring it was more family she began to walk over to the door. Then she saw Anderson step inside with her mother right behind him. All the music and voices around her went mute for a moment. The bottle in her room came back to her mind. Looking at Anderson walking through that door was as good as looking at a dead man. She watched as he hung his coat up but he hadn't seen her yet. Just as she was about to let Nate know he had arrived her mom called out to her from the door. "Nattalie!" Lilian rushed over to her.

"Hey momma. What's wrong?" Lilian looked upset.

"Uh, I'm not sure. But…. can I ask you something?" She pulled Nattalie into the kitchen.

"Mom what is it?" She placed her hands on Nattalie's shoulders.

"Anderson is in trouble." Nattalie froze.

"What do you mean?"

"I mean I got a call today from the police in Minnesota. They were looking for him." Nate walked into the kitchen. "Looking for who?" Lilian grabbed Nate's hand and led them both onto the patio. "Look I don't know all the details but the officer on the phone said that he's wanted for rape. I don't know what to do and I'm afraid to ask him if it's true."

"Ha… have you talked to his dad at all?" Nate asked.

"No not yet. I got the call right before I left to pick him up from the hotel. My brother has to know already. How else would the police know to call me? Or that he was even here?"

Nattalie was still frozen and afraid to say anything. Nate sat their mom down on the patio chair. "Listen even if he was innocent you can't hide him from the police. You gotta tell them where he's staying so they can investigate." Lilian nodded her head. "Okay but after the party. Your dad and Toni worked so hard to make tonight special. I don't wanna ruin it." They all nodded and agreed. Lilian went back inside while the twins stayed on the patio. Nattalie let out a sigh as if she'd been holding her breath the whole time. Nate breathed a sigh of relief. "This is great." He said. "You bet it is!" Nattalie agreed. "Somebody else ratted on him. So, when they find him dead, they'll figure it's suicide!" Nate was stunned. They had the biggest way out of committing murder, and she wanted to kill him anyway. "No Nattalie! We can just let mom turn him in!"

"Okay but we can still send him back to the hotel with the bottle. He'll take a drink I know it! I don't want him to just get jail time. I want him dead!" Nate's blood ran cold at the look in her eyes. She was much further gone than he'd realized. So rather than argue with a mad woman, he just went inside. Nattalie paced the patio floor for a few minutes before going inside. The music and dancing were still going strong. But her mind was far from the festivities. She watched as her mom sat in the corner with her knees shaking. While holding a glass of wine. Nattalie began to wonder if the family could bare a death at this point. Her thoughts had completely tuned out everything else in the room. Then she looked up to see Anderson looking right at her, smirking. Her body was frozen in one spot. Beads of sweat began to form on her brow and her breathing became labored. For a moment she was frightened but the fright quickly turned into rage. Her feet released themselves from the spot they were stuck in and headed to her bedroom. It was too early to give him the bottle to drink. But she was beginning to think that she wouldn't be able to carry on the rest of the evening without breaking down. Pacing back and forth in front of her bed she fought with herself. "Get it together Nattalie!" She said to herself. "Quit being soft! You have to do this." Her door began to slowly creep open and Anderson stepped into the room still smirking.

"Well aren't you happy to see me Nattie cake?"

"Don't call me that."

"Oh, come on now. We were so close at one point, weren't we? I've thought about you every day since the last time I was here." He kept walking toward her until her back was against the wall. His fingers wrapped around the soft curls in her hair and he leaned in to smell her perfume. "You always smelled so sweet." Pressing his body against hers she could feel his erection against her leg.

"Wait! Please…wait." She quickly pulled her emotions together, remembering what she had to do. Her voice had turned soft and flirty. "Uh ya know I've thought about you every day since you were last here too. Why don't we have a drink first?"

He backed away a little bit. "A drink?"

"Yes," She motioned her head toward the nightstand. "Everyone out there is pretty drunk anyway, I think. So why don't we have our own party in here?" Anderson looked at the bottle and then went to grab it. He pulled the cork out then looked around for a glass.

"No glasses?"

"Uh... we don't need a glass. We can just drink from the bottle." He nodded his head then turned the bottle up to take a drink. Fear and satisfaction swept over Nattalie like a wave. He took several gulps before offering it to her. "Oh, me and Nate were drinking earlier. I'll have some more later. You can drink some more if you want." He walked toward her with the bottle still in his hand. "You sure Nattie cake? Or can't I call you that?" He continued drinking as he pinned her body against the wall with his. Finally, he sat the bottle on her dresser and began grabbing at her breast. She could tell he'd been drinking even before he got there. The familiar smell of liquor oozed from his breath. He pulled her close to him and pulled up her skirt. "I missed you Nattie. Just let go for me." She was shaking uncontrollably with anger when he suddenly backed away. He was holding his stomach and moaning. "Wha..what's happening? Ahhhh!" He fell to his knees and his body shook. Nattalie pulled her skirt down and fixed her clothes. She walked over to him while he moaned even louder in pain. "Help!" He attempted to scream in a weak voice, but the music was too loud for anyone to hear him. Crouching down next to him as he now began to vomit, she whispered in his ear. "You're dying Anderson. You see, I've thought about you every day for a year and I've decided that you were right. There is no god. You know what else I discovered after that? I am god. So, you don't get to live in my world anymore." Anderson threw his head forward hard, knocking her in the forehead. She fell back and he stumbled out of the room as fast as he could. "Help! Help!" He stumbled his way through the crowd of people, now barely able to see. Nick ran to see what was wrong. "Anderson are you sick? What's wrong?" Anderson grabbed Nicks shirt. "It hurts. I need air." Nick took him out to the front porch. "Toni call 911 please!" No sooner than they stepped outside, several police cars pulled up in front of the house. "Dad!" Nate called out as he ran up to the house with Kelsey right behind him. "Let him go dad!" Nick was so confused. "What in hell is going on here? He needs help!" An officer approached them. "Are you Anderson Harris☐?" Anderson's eyes went cross and he collapsed. "Get a paramedic out here now!" The officer yelled. "Officer what's this about?" Nick asked. "You know this guy?"

Nick nodded. "Yea he's my nephew." "He has a warrant out for his arrest. Rape of a Sixteen-year-old girl." Nick's mind immediately went to Nattalie. The events of the past year flashed through his mind. How different she was after coming back from Minnesota. Her pregnancy and unwillingness to tell anyone who the father was. It all made sense in a moment. The paramedics sirens where up the street and Nick went inside to find his daughter. Who was staring out the front window with a peculiar grin on her face. Watching as Anderson was loaded into the ambulance.

Nick, Nathan, and Kelsey came rushing into the house after the ambulance took off down the street. "Nattie are you okay?" Nate stood watching her staring out of the window. "Nattie answer please." Nick said. She turned slowly toward him; her forehead was wrinkled as if she was solving a hard problem. Just as she was about to answer him, she noticed Kelsey was there.

"What's she doing here?"

"Don't get mad Nattie. It's my fault she's here. She helped me."

"Helped you? Are you kidding me?"

"Now hang on a minute! I don't know what in hell you two are talking about, but somebody better tell me what's going on now!" Nick realized that there was still a house full of people and they had an audience. "Everyone the party is over. I'm sorry and I wish I could explain but I don't know what's happening." The guest started to leave, and Lilian came into the living room with Toni. "It's my fault Nick." Lilian's eyes were red from crying. "What do you mean it's your fault?"

"I got a call earlier from an officer in Minnesota. They were looking for Anderson. Something about rape charges. I didn't know what to tell them. His flight hadn't gotten in yet and…. and..."

"So, you thought you'd wait until the whole family was here to have him arrested?" Nick snapped.

"No, no! I didn't tell them anything. I was going to wait till after the party to say something."

They all looked at each other puzzled until Toni spoke up. "Well if you didn't call the police then who did?" They looked around at each other for a moment until a voice called out. "I did." Kelsey, who was almost standing behind Nate at this point, stepped out in front of him. Trying to avoid eye contact with Nattalie, she hung her head and said. "I did. I called the police."

"You? How did you know?" Lilian asked.

"Why are you here in the first place? I told you to stay away!"

"Be quiet Nattalie." Nick snapped again.

Kelsey stood with her arms folded and her head still lowered. "I came to check on Nate when I overheard him and Nattalie talking to their mom about it in the kitchen." She turned to Nate with tears in her eyes. "I'm sorry but when I heard her say the cops were looking for Anderson, I figured it was the perfect way to get rid of him without killing him!" Lillian and Toni gasped. Nick shook his head. "What did you say?" Kelsey realized that she'd said too much but couldn't think fast enough to cover it up. Nick stepped right up to Kelsey. "Tell me what you said again." She was shaking all over and her heart was pounding in her throat. "I…. I didn't mean it." Nick had had enough. "Go home Kelsey. I'll get to the bottom of this myself." Kelsey turned to Nate with tears rolling down her face. "I'm sorry Nate. I really wanted to help you. Both of you." She ran as fast as she could out the door and down the street.

The Bottom of This

Nathan, Nattalie, Lillian and Toni all sat in the living room while Nick paced the floor. He had demanded everyone to sit down but hadn't said a word in about ten minutes. He began to walk around the house snatching Christmas decorations off the walls. Even the huge "MERRY CHRISTMAS" banner that hung in the dining room came down. None of them had seen him so angry in a very long time. No one dared speak. Finally, he came back into the living room. "Alright. Somebody better start talking. What has been going on around here?" Nate cleared his throat and looked to see if Nattalie had even budged. No reaction from her at all just folded arms with a look of annoyance on her face. Nate cleared his throat again. "Ummm, dad. Anderson just wasn't feeling too well and..," Nick walked closer to him. "Don't even think about lying to me son. Now explain what Kelsey was talking about! Did you try to kill Anderson?" Nate stood up. "No dad." Nick walked over to Nattalie and sat down next to her. She avoided eye contact, but he turned her face gently toward his. "Did you?" She was silent. "Nattalie, did you try to kill Anderson?" She remained silent. Toni and Lilian both were crying. "No answer? I ask you if you tried to murder you cousin and I get no answer? What did he do to you? Tell me Nattalie." Nick pleaded with her, but she just got angry. She jumped up from the couch. "What does it matter? He's a rapist. That's why the cops were here right? He deserved it. You should all be thanking me!" She through her arms up into the air as if celebrating. Lillian tried to reason with her. "Sweetheart sit down and let's talk. If he hurt you, we can help."

"Help? Help? Oh, now you want to help. You know first you abandon us and move states away. Then the first chance we got to visit you, you dumped us at the house of our atheist, alcoholic cousin! Aunt Chassy was so sick we shouldn't have even been in that f@#$ household! But your new boyfriend or whatever was more important to you. Actually no. You were more important to you than us." Lilian sobbed uncontrollably. "I'm so sorry baby. I... I was so wrong. Look what I've done to you." She cried hard and long. But Nattalie just looked at her. She knew she'd been trying to be a better mom over the past year but at that moment she didn't care. What was done was done and now everyone knew who was truly to blame.

Nattalie stomped off down the hall to her room and slammed the door. The rest of the family just sat there in tears, trying to wrap their minds around what they had just heard. "Son, did you know anything about this?" Nick asked as he took Nate by the shoulders. Nate wanted to cover for himself, but he couldn't go on with it anymore. "Yea.... yea I did." The tears broke from his eyes in waves. "Son why? Why didn't you come to me?" He held tighter onto his shoulders. "I couldn't dad! Nattalie needed me. I failed her before when I left her back in Minnesota. I couldn't fail her again." Nick pulled his son in and held him tight as he cried like he'd never seen him cry before. "It's okay son. Look we will get through this, but I need you to tell me everything. Your sister is in a lot of trouble if Anderson dies. You gotta tell me what happened." Nate wiped his face and nodded his head. "Okay but you'd better sit-down dad." Then he looked at Lillian. "Mom, can you handle this right now?" She wiped her eyes and sat up straight. "My bad choices set her on this path. I can at least listen to the damage I've caused." Toni grabbed Nicks hand and they all sat down to hear what had been happening to their daughter over the past year. A series of tears, gasp and looks of shock ensued as Nate told them all he knew. Nattalie's rape, the mystery father of her baby. The mental torment she'd endured for that whole year was apparent to them all through his words. After about thirty minutes, Nate closed with "I just wanted to help her. I'm sorry I wasn't strong enough to tell her, no." The room was silent, and everyone was still in disbelief at what they'd heard. A sudden feeling of relief came over Nate. He sat back onto the couch and sighed a deep sigh. Although he knew Nattalie might never forgive him. It still felt better to tell everyone the truth. The silence had become deafening. Nick finally spoke up. "Somebody has to go to the hospital and see about Anderson." Nate jumped up. "Dad! Shouldn't we be more concerned about Nattalie?" It was shocking to him that Anderson would be his dads first concern. "If Anderson dies then Nattalie could be charged with murder! We need a lawyer as it is. But we need to know what we're dealing with. Murder or attempted murder." Nick looked at Lillian who was still so stunned she'd barely moved. "Lillian, he's your nephew. I know it's hard but could you possibly...." Lillian began shaking her head before Nick could even get the question out. Toni, who felt more like an outsider in the situation, spoke up. "I'll go Nick. I'll find out what I can and call you from the hospital." He nodded his head and then walked her to her car. When the door shut,

Nate sat down next to Lillian. "Mom, we don't have to tell on her." Her eyes were so blurred from crying it was hard for her to focus on his face.

"Son, if Anderson dies, they'll figure out he was poisoned and come looking for someone. Even if he lives, she's still in trouble because he's sure to tell! Did you two give any real though to this at all?"

"I don't think she cared mom. In fact, I know she didn't care. Not about us or herself. Just about her revenge and I fell right into it." Nick came back into the house. "Alright I'm going to call my lawyer first thing in the morning. I don't think there's any point in trying to get anything out of Nattalie tonight but I'm going to check on her." He paused for a moment before heading down the hall and looked back at Nate and Lillian still sitting on the couch. "She's still my daughter." He said as if reminding himself. Then headed to her room. He tapped on the door and called her name. "Nattalie? Honey it's… it's dad." He pushed the door open gently and peaked inside. A brush of wind blew across his face from the open window in her room. She was gone.

"Nate! Lillian! Get in here!"

"What dad?"

"She's gone. Where would she go?"

Nick was so confused. He paced her bedroom floor trying to think of where she might have gone to. The phone started ringing. They all raced to answer it, but Nate got it first. "Hello hello.... wait what? How did she get there? Never mind we're coming." Nate hung up. "Nattalie's at the hospital. That was Toni." He grabbed a sweatshirt from his room and threw it on over his head.

"Why would she go there?"

"For the same reason Toni went there. To see if Anderson lives or dies. Now come on dad☐, I'll drive."

At the hospital, Nattalie sat in the waiting room near Toni. But tried very hard to pretend she wasn't there. She read the horoscopes from a fashion magazine and smiled to herself. "Your life is headed in a new direction." She read from the article out loud and laughed. "Can they get anymore vague with this crap?" She said to herself. The way she sat reading as if nothing had happened made Toni's blood run cold. She wanted to say something to her but was almost afraid to. Suddenly Nattalie closed the magazine and slammed it on the waiting room table. "Where is that doctor? Geez how long does it take to know if someone it dead?" Her arms folded tight across her chest and she slouched down in the chair. "Is that why you came?" Toni asked. "You came to see if you succeeded?" Nattalie smirked at Toni but said nothing else. Just a moment later Nick, Nate and Lillian came into the waiting room. Toni was relieved to see them. She threw her arms around Nick and kissed his face. No one knew what to say to Nattalie. They all awkwardly began to sit down just as the doctor walked in. Everyone got up to hear the news. "Are you the family of Anderson Harris?" The doctor asked. "I am his Aunt. He's staying with me for the week. Is he alright?" Lillian answered. "He's suffered some internal injury, but we were able to insert a tube through the nose and suction out what remained in his stomach. It appears he had ingested poison. Although we are running more test to find out exactly what it was that he ingested."

Lillian looked to see if Nattalie would react, but she never even flinched. Her expression was almost frozen. Her soft features didn't match the hardness that pierced through her eyes. Like a delicate painting in too bold of a frame. "He can't talk now but unfortunately you'll have to wait to be in contact with him at all. The police are standing guard by his room right now and…."

Two police officers walked into the room. "Excuse me folks. I'm Detective Alvarez and this is my partner Detective Richmond. I understand you are the family of Mr. Harris." Lillian nodded. "I am his aunt." Detective Alvarez looked through his notes. "Are you Lillian Blythe?" She nodded. "Yes I am." He closed his note pad. "Ms. Blythe I was told that the police up in Minnesota contacted you about your nephew." Her heart started beating a little faster. "That's right. They did." Her palms became sweaty. "Well I'm glad you called. He's been accused of three different rapes over the past two years. But the young ladies always back out before the court date. This last victim doesn't seem like she has any intention of backing out. She wants justice. But we'd like to ask you all a few questions, Ms. Blythe. "Well I don't know anything. I'm just as shocked as anyone else." Her mouth felt dry and it was difficult for her to form her words. "It's not about the case in Minnesota. It's about his current condition. The doctors say he was poisoned. You know anything about that?" They were all stuck for words. Like deer in head lights they stood there trying to think of something to say. Except Nattalie. She stood there with her arms folded, tapping her foot on the floor. Her mind felt like it was slipping into a fog. He was alive and she was angry. Within seconds she could smell the stench of liquor and sweat from Anderson's palms on her skin. His voice was in her head like an echo and her stomach turned. All of a sudden, she collapsed to the floor and screamed out.

"It was me!"

"Nattalie, oh my god! Nattalie please, please. Don't say anything else just let daddy take you home sweetie."

"It was me officer!"

They all began to sob. Nick folded her in his arms and cried on her head. Her body was so numb she felt as if she could float away. "I'm ending this. They'll catch me anyway eventually." She gave a sinister laugh. Tears rolled down her cheeks. "It's over. I failed. He's still alive and my life still feels like death!" Lillian whaled as the police put her in hand cuffs and read her her rights. Nick sat in a chair holding Toni while Nate beat his fist into a wall. They led her to the back of a police car and what was left of her disappeared down the street in a haze of blue and red lights.

Just and Unjust

It was five thirty in the morning and Nattalie's eyes began to open. The lights were a bright white and the room was spinning. "Nate!! Dad!" She called out for them to help her. She could barely see. "Nate!" Then an unfamiliar alarm went off and she shot up out of bed. But it wasn't her bed. "Where am I?" She wiped her eyes to try and clear up her vision. Then looked down confused about the tan jump suit she was wearing. The strange alarm sounded again and then a heavy clanging sound. Now she remembered where she was. The clanging sound was her cell door unlocking. Up until that moment everything had felt like a dream. She walked out into a hall where dozens of other women wearing the same tan jump suit were lining up. Her thoughts raced over the events of the past few months. She wasn't even sure how long she'd been there. "Hey curls!" Another inmate called out. Nattalie wasn't sure if she was talking to her although she was looking right at her. "Hey, you feeling better? Or you black out again?" The inmate laughed. Slowly she began to recognize her. "Patty?" She shook her head. "Yea it's me! Hey, you need to go to the shrink or something. You been here like three months and every other week you forget where you are. That ain't right." It was all clear again. "I'm sorry. I don't know what's wrong with me." Patty had been there for two years and had seen all sorts of mental breakdowns. "No big deal ya know. It's hard to adjust to being here." Patty was only four years older than she was. It was a cold place for such a young woman to be. But from the moment she saw Nattalie walk into that place, she felt as if she needed to protect her. Later that afternoon Nattalie was in her cell when a guard came to see her. "Let's go Blythe. You have a visitor." After spending all morning trying to mentally piece together the past few months, that was the best news she could have gotten. Being led handcuffed to the visitor's room was humiliating. The guard never looked her in the face. He may as well have been leading a dog outside. They stopped at the doors where she could see her dad, mom and brother sitting waiting for her. Those cuffs couldn't come off fast enough. When she walked in, she ran to her brother's arms. "No touching!" A guard shouted at her. The rules certainly were not at the fore front of her thought. They all sat down at the round cafeteria style tables.

"Oh, baby how you holding up?" Lilian asked.

"I don't really know mom. I woke up this morning and I didn't know where I was. I was confused and…"

"I know baby I know. The same thing happened last month remember?"

"No not really. Should I ask to see a doctor?"

"You already have sweetie. Nick said."

"Well what did they say?"

"Sis, you have PTSD remember? It's been happening for a while, but it's gotten worse since you've been here."

"I remember now. But wait? How long do I have to be here again?" They all looked at each other not wanting to have to break the news to her again. "Sweetie you got fifteen years. All but five years were suspended. Now you may be able to get out in three with good behavior, but you'll be on probation for three years after that. If at any time you violate that probation the judge could make you finish the whole fifteen years." Her mind began to recall the court hearing and the look on her dad's face when he first heard it. She sighed deep as she buried her face in her hands.

☐ "I remember now. What about Anderson?"

"Sweetie we don't need to talk about him right now."

"Where is he dad?"

"Sweetie please. Why don't we talk about something else."

"What else is there to talk about dad? I'm in jail!"

"Nattie…please."

"Where is he?" Nate decided to speak up before Nattalie got too upset. "He's dead sis."

"What? How? The doctor said he would live! He died anyway?"

"He killed himself Nattie. He killed himself. After that girl pressed charges the other girls decided to testify too. He shot himself the day before this court hearing." It felt as though the blood had drained from her face. She had been angry because she'd failed to get rid of him. But in the end, he destroyed himself. At that moment it was as if someone had broken the dam to her emotions and they swept over her in one big wave. She cried and cried with her head on the table until she could hardly catch her breath. They all tried to comfort her but every time they touched her the guard yelled at them. "Ma..mom, Da… dad. I'm so sorry. I hated him so, so much. I let him ruin my life." Her body was shivering, and she couldn't control her crying. "Visiting hours are over!" The guard came over to take her back to her cell. "Wait! No! Please! I can't be here!! Wait!" Two guards had to drag her out of the room. Nate held Lillian back as she tried to grab hold of Nattalie's arm. "We love you Nattie!" Nate called out while holding his crying mother. "We love you!"

The walk back to her cell didn't seem real. She felt like she was in a haze unable to see anything but what was directly in front of her. Finally, she was back inside her cell. The sound of the large metal door locking seemed to make the haze disappear. That sound let her know it was real. Looking out the small window on the door she could see other inmates looking out of their cells too. Some were older and others very young. She wondered how long they had been there and furthermore, how they had survived without going mad. She had only recalled the events of the past few months within the last hour. Already she felt like she was going mad. "Hey curls." Nattalie was startled by the voice that was suddenly in the cell with her. "Ha-ha! Dang girl you must be having a real rough day. But it just got better. Looks like we're cell mates." Nattalie rubbed her eyes a little. "Patty?" Patty laid back on the bottom bunk. "Oh my god girl. You killin' me today. You need to see the doc for real. What he say last time?" Nattalie shrugged her shoulders. "I don't know. But I remember you now. You're always nice to me." Patty laughed. "Yea it's me. You think about what I asked you the other week? Or you don't remember?" After seeing the confused look on Nattalie's face she decided to just ask again.

"Okay well you wanna sign up for chapel? Tomorrow is the last day to get your name on the list."

"Oh, I don't believe in God. But thanks for the offer I guess."

"It ain't like regular church though. I mean there's like singers from Life Christian Fellowship that come. But it's not like regular preaching and stuff."

"I went to that church when I was a kid. But if it's not regular preaching then what is it like then? Just singing?"

"Nah. The dude that's coming isn't a preacher. He's called an apologist."

"What's he sorry for?" Patty laughed loudly.

"Hey, I said the same thing when I first heard it. An apologist is a person who like defends what they believe and stuff. Like with logic ya□ know."

"Logic? What's so logical about a God who stands by and watches people get hurt?"

"I don't know girl. But you could even ask him that question."

"What? No way."

"Yea, yea. There's like a question and answer after his talk. You can ask him anything for real."

"Look I doubt anyone could explain away why my life has sucked. I'm really not in the mood to hear about some cosmic sky daddy who supposedly loves me."

"Alright girl. Your loss. At the least it's a chance to get out of this stupid cell. Hear some music and sorta feel normal for a couple of hours. I mean come on; it won't kill you. Even if it is against your good atheist values." They both laughed.

"Ok, I guess. Just to get out of this cell though."

"Cool, cool."

The room was filled front to back by the time Nattalie and Patty arrived. There was still about fifteen minutes left before it started. They looked around for a closer place to sit but only found two end seats separated by two rows. "Looks like we won't sit together if we don't wanna be in the back. That cool with you curls?" Nattalie shrugged. "Yea I guess." No sooner had they sat down four people dressed in matching T-Shirts with Love Fellowship logos came to the microphones. "Good evening sisters. Please stand to your feet as we just take a moment to worship." The sound quality of prison microphones was horrible and pretty distracting. Until a young tattooed man sat at a keyboard and began to play a very familiar worship song. Nattalie knew the song well. They sang it often when she was growing up and almost instinctively, she began to sing along. After a few minutes she started wishing she was back in church as a kid so she could ask for a mint. The old church mothers carried mints as if it were a commandment. There was a calm in that place she'd never felt before. The room was filled with such beautiful sounds and the lead singers voice was enough to bring anyone to tears. She reasoned through the warm comforting feelings. "It's just nostalgia." She thought. But she continued singing to the point of tears. Again, she thought. "It's just the pretty music." Finally, worship ended and although she sat down quickly. She really didn't want it to stop.

The jail Chaplain took the mic. "Hello everyone. Thank you all for signing up to be here. Our speaker tonight is no stranger to us here. He travels the world giving evidence for Christianity and encouraging believers to be well equipped to defend the faith. At the end we will have a question and answer session which is my favorite part. So, it is my pleasure to present to you your speaker for the evening, Dr. Thomas Cortez." The room applauded as a rather young-looking Hispanic man walked onto the stage. For some reason Nattalie expected an older person with a beard and a few more miles on his face to be the speaker. It was a pleasant surprise. He took the mic and began to speak. "I am always so humbled to be invited to speak here. The question of the existence of God is the most important question in life. Last time we presented the arguments for the creation of the universe and design. Tonight, we are going to look at the moral argument. Where did this morality business come from and how do we know what it is? The British writer and theologian C.S Lewis was a former atheist. C.S Lewis said, "My argument against God was that the universe seemed so cruel and unjust. But how had I got this idea of just and unjust? A man does not call a line crooked unless he has some idea of a straight line. One of the biggest objections to the existence of God is the problem of evil." If there is a good God, then where is he? Why doesn't he wave his magic wand and stop all the evil in the world? Well first of all, where have we gotten this idea of evil from in the first place? The minute you start to make complaints about evil, you presuppose an objective standard of good. But what is that standard? I've heard atheist say that they are their own standard and they don't need any God or book to tell them how to be good people. I actually agree with that. You don't need to be told what is good and what is bad. You know it! But how do you know it? Furthermore, if each person sets his own standard of good and evil then how do you complain when another person has a standard that's not the same as yours? If I say to myself, hey I like that guy's coat, and I deem it beneficial to myself to steal that coat. Who says I'm wrong? If my moral compass is pointing at myself. Then why can't I make up my own rules? On an atheistic, naturalistic worldview, you simply can't justify calling anything good or evil. Jeffrey Dahmer the notorious serial killer was quoted in saying, "If it all happens naturalistically, what's the need for a God? Can't I set my own rules? Who owns me? I own myself."

Nattalie's mind immediately went back to the night she poisoned Anderson. It was like this guy was in her head. He'd pinned her thoughts exactly. She was glued to her seat as Dr. Cortez continued to speak.

"There must be a standard outside of humanity by which to measure right and wrong if we are going to say that anything is right or wrong. That standard is found in the very nature of God. Without it, everything is just a matter of opinion."

The presentation went on and with a lineup of slide shows and videos. But the question and answer portion of the evening couldn't come fast enough. Nattalie sat with her arms folded tight. She heard everything Dr. Cortez had said but was getting angrier as the night went on. It still didn't make sense to her. "If there is a God and our standards come from him then does evil come from him too?" She thought. The question and answer period couldn't come soon enough.

"Thank you all so much for being here tonight." Everyone applauded as Dr. Cortez moved a microphone stand closer to center aisle. "If you have any questions please line up at the mic. We'll have about thirty minutes for questions." Nattalie was already out of her seat before the mic was set up. She was the first in line with quite a few people behind her. "Yes ma'am! Please come closer to the mic so we can hear you." Dr. Cortez motioned for her to come closer. Nattalie tried to control her emotions as she spoke. "Yes, uhhhh." She took a deep breath and her face was red from fighting back tears. "I get that right or wrong has to be based on something. But if God is the standard of good, why does he let bad things happen? Why doesn't he destroy all the evil in the world?" Her bottom lip quivered as Dr. Cortez came a little closer to the edge of the stage. "Miss, I know we're in a jail, but I'll ask anyway because I don't know what landed you here. Have you ever done an evil thing in your life? Or something that was just plain wrong? Something that hurt someone else in word or in action? Even if you felt they deserved it?" Nattalie thought about the poison she'd put in Andersons drink. The pleasure she felt when he collapsed on the floor and how they had come so close to carrying out murder. Here she was in jail and asking about evil as if it didn't apply to her. She felt a bit stupid in the moment. "I…I guess I have." Dr. Cortez nodded. "Then if God destroyed all the evil in the world, you could be on that list. I could be on that list. I've done what is evil in God's eyes many times. However, when I have felt it unfair that someone else live after the wrong they have done, I remember the wrong I've done. The beautiful thing about God is that He gives us all the same grace and the same chance to get it right while we are alive." Nattalie folded her arms and tried to respond but couldn't. Dr. Cortez, seeing that there was something more, spoke instead. "What's your name?" He asked. "Nattalie." She said in almost a whisper. "Nice to meet you. Nattalie, God loves you. Even after you did evil, He loves you and affords you the same chance for redemption as everyone else. It's your choice to take what he's offering." Nattalie cut her eyes at him sharp. "Look I hear you but you gotta admit that some wrongs are worse than others. Some wrongs do permanent damage, and some do minor damage. Why should someone who hurts people get the same grace as someone who stole a cookie from the store?" Shouldn't the punishment fit the crime?" Her heart was beating fast and she felt as if she would cry again. "Yes, the punishment should fit the crime. But we are all guilty of something. So, no matter what type of crime we've committed, it's still a crime. We all deserve punishment. Still he gives us grace and chance after chance so long as we live to repent. I didn't deserve it but I'm grateful." She nodded; she wasn't sure how to feel about his answer. "Thank you. I'd better sit down." She turned to go back to her seat. "Wait one second Nattalie." Dr. Cortez motioned for the chaplain to come over. "There's a book that I donated several of to the library here about a year ago. It's called 'A problem of evil.' Chaplain Dean here can get it for you if you're interested." She shrugged her shoulders. "Yea, I guess so." She returned to her seat, wishing she'd never got up to speak. She didn't want to read any book and she was angry that she should be guilty of anything after what Anderson had done to her.

She laid in her bunk that night and couldn't sleep at all. Her mind replayed Dr. Cortez's words but as soon as they would start to make sense, her anger would take over. "God is good, but he gives grace to rapist? How?" She tossed and turned and talked to herself, out loud at times. "Hey, be quiet down there." An irritated Patty groaned. "Sorry Patty." Patty leaned over the side of the top bunk. "What's wrong with you? You been mumbling for the past hour." Nattalie sat up a little. "I just don't get it. Like how could a good God give grace to people who hurt others?" Patty sighed. "Aren't you in here for hurting somebody?" She groaned feeling annoyed. "Yea, yea. I am." Patty sat up too. "Okay then. God has grace for you too. That's what Cortez was tryna tell you. You not listening cus you so hurt and angry. But you gotta let that go and live girl." Nattalie laid back down and pulled the covers over herself. "I don't even believe in God so none of this matters." Patty leaned over the top bunk again.

"Hey, what happened to the dude that raped you?"

"He killed himself."

"Aww man. Really? Hey check this out. If there ain't no God, then dude just got off free and clear. I'd rather believe that there's justice in the end than none at all. Now good night and be quiet curls."

☐Nattalie kept quiet, but that thought was the most unsettling of all. She'd plotted for weeks to get justice for what Anderson had done. If God really didn't exist, then he really did just get away with it.

The next day Nattalie decided to go to the prison library. She walked into the dusty old room and began to look for the title Dr. Cortez had recommended. "Hello Nattalie!" Suddenly a voice called her name and startled her. "Oh Chaplain, it's you. You're the librarian too?" He chuckled. "No, I just come in to help organize the place from time to time. I've always had an affection for books." He sniffed the air. "Nothing like the smell of them, especially brand-new ones." He patted a cart of very new looking books. "I know what you mean." She sighed deeply. "I loved books too." The Chaplain furrowed his brow.

"What? You don't love them anymore?"

"I mean I do. I just haven't enjoyed one in a long while."

She walked along the aisle and ran her fingers across the spines of books on the shelves. "Well as far as I can tell you're still alive. You can always rekindle that love. Oh, I almost forgot!" He walked over to the religious book section. "Here's that book Dr. Cortez recommended for you." He placed it into her hands. "Thank you. Ummm.... can I ask you something?" He motioned to a small table. "Of course. Why don't we sit down?" They sat down on the hard, wooden chairs at a table riddled with graffiti. "What's on your mind Nattalie?" She looked at the book title before she spoke. "Why do you believe in God? I mean you've obviously dedicated your life to your religion. But you can't even see the thing you're worshiping. So how can you believe in it?" He folded his hands in front of him.

"I believe in God because I find good reason to believe that He exists."

"Oh, come on! I mean isn't this whole thing based on faith?"

"Yes, it is!"

"Ok so isn't that believing something without any evidence for it?"

"Well that depends on what definition of faith you're appealing to."

"What do you mean? Isn't there only one definition?"

"In English, yes. But it's different in Greek."

"How?"

"The English definition is just as you said. Believing something without evidence. In the Greek, which is the language the New testament was written in, the word we translate into 'Faith' is 'Pistis.' It means trust. Wait just a minute." He got up to grab a Bible from a bookshelf. After blowing some dust off of it, he sat down and began to read.

"Now faith is the substance of things hoped for, the evidence of things not seen. That's Hebrews 11:1. I want you to note the word 'evidence' Nattalie. Biblical faith doesn't mean you believe something without evidence. Biblical faith is when you believe what you have evidence for. You may not be able to see God with your eyes, but the evidence of his existence is all around us. In fact, the evidence for his existence, is us."

"But how do we know that for sure? I mean what about evolution and stuff? Can't it all just be chance?"

The chaplain began to laugh. "Well if all of our bodily organs and brain functions are the product of chance, how can you even trust anything you think at all?" He shook his head. "The human body is a wondrous thing. From the way broken bones can heal themselves, to the way babies are formed in the womb. It's all too magnificent to be accidental and I don't think it is unreasonable to believe that a mind was behind it all."

"I see. I mean I hear you but…"

"How long do have left here?"

"I'm eligible for parole in three years."

"That's enough time." He got up again and walked over to another aisle of books. This time returning with several in his hand. "Here, I want you to read these."

"What's all this?"

"They are books on the arguments for the existence of God, reliability of the New Testament and some early church history."

"It'll take me all three years to read through this."

☐ "Do you want to know the truth? Or are you happy in your unbelief?"

She didn't quite know how to answer. Doubt and anger had become a comfortable position for her. She could be mad and do as she pleased. But now a new question had been presented to her and she had to ask herself, "do I want to know the truth?" After a few seconds had passed by she answered, "yes I do."

"Good. Start with this one."

He handed her a book and she read the title out loud. "From effect to cause. Classic arguments for the existence of God."

"I'll meet you here after lunch on Saturday's so we can discuss what you've read so far."

She felt a bit overwhelmed but was very curious. She'd never known that real scholars actually argue for God's existence. "Okay, you got a deal." With that they shook hands and parted ways.

The first week had passed and Nattalie's head felt as if it was going to explode. She'd read through the arguments for the beginning of the universe, for design and the moral arguments. Including some essays, she'd found in the library by an Oxford Scholar. It was all fascinating to her and frustrating at the same time. Especially the design argument. Trying to pin the existence of something as complicated as DNA on mere chance was putting her brain in a knot. It was the most compelling to her. She laid in her bunk that Friday night thinking about all she'd read so far. Her leg itched, so she reached down to scratch it. Then she reached down to touch the same spot again. She sat up, then laid back down. She opened her mouth and closed it again. Whatever action she willed her body to do, it did. "There's nothing random about the control I have over my body. I can intentionally sit up or lay down or scratch. How could that happen if my brain function was accidental?" She thought to herself as she sat up and down again. "My muscles are working together. But how? Maybe we are designed." Flopping back down on the bed she became frustrated again. The night couldn't pass quickly enough. The next day she was supposed to see the Chaplain.

After lunch she hurried to the library. As soon as she walked in the door, she saw the Chaplain already sitting at the little table. As soon as she sat down, she asked a question. "If we really are designed then how come people get sick? Or are born with disabilities and stuff? What's up with kids having cancer if we are designed?" The Chaplain gave his usual chuckle.

"Well hello Nattalie, glad you could make it."

"Come on, you gotta admit that doesn't sound very designed."

"Oh no? You ever own something that quit working after a while or even came not working right out of the box?"

"Yea. I got a stereo once for Christmas that quit working after a week."

"Did that mean that no one designed the stereo?"

"No. I guess it doesn't."

"Well, just because something doesn't work the way we think it should, doesn't mean it wasn't designed."

She leaned back in her chair and let out a deep sigh. "Okay but if God is perfect then why design people who break down? Why disease and starvation and..." She sighed again and leaned forward on the table. "I just don't get it." He patted her hand. "Nattalie, our bodies weren't made to live forever on this earth. We were made for eternity and in this fallen world there are many illnesses and unfortunate occurrences that make life hard. But just because things don't work the way we'd like them to, doesn't mean that there was never a designer." He smiled a curious smile. "What are you smiling at?" She asked. "I was just thinking about your stereo. The one you said quit working after a week." She shrugged her shoulders. "Yea, what about it?" "Well I was just thinking. Some person took time to design it and then maybe sold his design to a stereo company. The design itself probably wasn't faulty. Perhaps some overworked and under paid employee at the factory messed it up." They both giggled a little bit. "Come to think of it. There's always some warning about some medication or food product that turns out to be harmful. We do a lot to harm ourselves you know?" Nattalie nodded her head. "Yea I get that. But it still doesn't explain why God lets people hurt other people." The Chaplain looked at his watch. "That's the drawback of creating free will creatures. They are free to make bad choices as well as good ones. Weren't you free to make whatever choice landed you here?" She'd almost forgotten where she was. Her mouthed gaped open. "Now I'm not trying to be rude. It's just interesting how we as humans always think of the sins of others as being the worst and never our own." He looked at his watch again. "I have to run now. I will see you next Saturday if you're still willing to continue." He stood up from the little table. She stood up along with him. "Yes, I'm still willing." She hung her head "I think I get it now." He placed his hand on her shoulder. "There's grace for us all. You just have to take the gift that God is offering you." With those words he turned and walked out of the little library.

The following weeks were a collage of details in Nattalie's mind. She didn't see people but rather the smalls things that were on and around the person. The buttons on the guard's uniforms. How someone somewhere sewed them on one by one and spaced them just right to attach to the other side of the shirt. The guns and holsters on their hips. She thought, "Now if someone told me that a factory exploded and a holster that fit that gun perfectly was created from the explosion by chance, I'd think they were crazy." The draw strings on her fellow in-mates jump suits. The chain linked fence around the prison yard and the barbed wire over the top of it. Everything she saw was made and with a specific intention. "Then why not us?" She said out loud as she banged her hand on the table. Everyone at her lunch table stopped and looked at her. "Hey curls. What's wrong with you?" Patty leaned in and whispered.

"I'm sorry. I guess I was thinking out loud."

"You've been having those blackouts?" Nattalie shook her head. "Nope. I actually haven't. I just uhhh…" Nattalie looked down at her tray and began to cry. "Hey curls, what's the matter?" Patty put her hand on Nattalie's shoulder.

"I think I get it Patty."

"What girl? What do you get?"

☐She buried her face in her hands for a few seconds and cried a little more. "I'm a creation. Someone wanted me here. I don't know why but I want to know."

Over the passing months Nattalie continued seeing the Chaplain on Saturday's and she read more and more books. Some days felt like a tug of war between her anger and her logic. Still she kept meeting him and kept learning. On a Wednesday afternoon, she walked out onto the prison yard and the sky seemed to be particularly blue. The sound of the birds chirping really sounded like a song. Even the brisk fall air felt like it was wrapping itself around her and she was in a sudden state of awe. At that moment she closed her eyes and prayed. "God, I believe you're really there now. I still don't quite get it all but if you made me then you can fix me. So please whatever you want to do, do it."

A week later, a guard was escorting Nattalie to the visitation room. After taking off her handcuffs, she joined her mom, dad, and her brother at a table. The smile on her face was huge and rather unexpected. "Hey sweetie. How you hanging in there?" Her dad asked. "I'm making it. Really I am." Nate sat next to her but would barely look at her.

"What's the matter Nate?" She asked

"I just hate that you're here. It's my fault. All of it. I didn't protect you and..."

"No, it's not your fault. I made my own decisions and then guilt tripped you into helping me. I meant it when I said I'm making it and I'm gonna get out of here one day."

☐She looked at all of their faces, confused at her optimism. "Nattalie. Are you sure you're okay?" Her mom asked. "Yea mom. I mean it gets lonely and I miss you guys but somehow, I feel better than I have in a long time. I have peace. Don't really know how to explain it but I'm good." They all felt a strange relief at her words. For the next hour they filled her in on what was going on back home and made plans for when she would be with them. At moments they were laughing so much it felt more like Saturday nights at home when she and Nate were little. Finally visiting hours were over and the guard came to take her back. As he walked her back out, Nate called out to her. "I love you Nattie cake!" Nattalie looked backed at her brother's tearing eyes. And smiled. "I love you too."

Looking Forward

"I wish I could say that the rest of her prison stay was easy, but it wasn't. It was hard. Even with the new hope that she had found it was a long journey out of that dark place she had been in. Eventually, after months of reading the scholars arguments and looking into the facts around Christianity, she was led out by the light of the gospel of Jesus Christ. It is because he met her in that low place that I stand before you today. Having blossomed and grown from that scared and bitterly angry young girl, I can feel nothing but gratefulness. Thank you all for being here tonight." The audience stood to its feet and applauded. Nattalie closed her notebook and looked to her right to see if her husband was there. He blew a kiss and mouthed an "I love you" in her direction. When the applause had died down a bit, she spoke into the microphone again. "We will have a brief Q&A if anyone would like to ask any questions. A few people lined up behind a microphone stand in the center aisle. One by one they stepped up to ask their questions. Some had questions about her time in jail. Others had theological questions relating to her other books. After about thirty minutes, someone signaled to her that it was time to wrap it up. "Well it looks like we only have time for one more question." An elderly woman approached the microphone. "Yes, what's your name." Nattalie asked. The woman cleared her throat. "Hello my name is Ruthy. I was wondering, how your mom was doing?" Nattalie was surprised. No one had ever asked about her mom specifically before.

"My mom? Well she's doing fine. I just saw her a few months ago."

"That's good to hear. The reason I asked is because I can relate to the type of person she was. She had a lot of pain and she bled on others because she never healed. I know what that's like, and I just wanted to know that you two were doing good still."

"Yes ma'am. She's come a long way. We both have."

"What about your dad and your brother? Did your dad ever marry that nice lady Toni?"

"As a matter of fact, he did. My brother has edited my last two books and my dad and Toni are retired now."

She could tell this news made Ruthy very happy. Just as Ruthy was about to thank Nattalie for her time, she asked another question. "Oh, one more thing. How were things once you got out of prison? Was it hard to adjust?" Nattalie's smile left briefly as she lowered her head. She looked back up to see a curious Ruthy waiting for her answer. "Well to tell you the truth, that's a whole other story." Ruthy gave a little laugh. "Well I'm looking forward to hearing it one day. God certainly is faithful." Nattalie nodded in agreement "Yes, he certainly is." Ruthy thanked her and walked away from the microphone. "That's all the time we have for tonight. Thank you again for your hospitality and God Bless you all. The auditorium applauded as Nattalie exited the stage toward her husband. He hugged her tight and kissed her face.

"I told you it would be fine babe."

"Yes, and it was. I have a new idea now."

"Oh really, what's that?"

"I want to do a new book but first I want to take a long vacation."

"Okay, how long we talking? A few weeks?"

"A few months actually."

"Wow, okay. How many months you thinking?"

"About seven and a half."

"That's oddly specific, honey."

"Well we're going to need time to prepare for the baby."

Josh was frozen as his mind processed what she had just said. Nattalie stood before him softly rubbing her stomach and smirking at him.

"Baby? Really?"

"Yes, really."

He picked her up and spun her around backstage. Nattalie was overwhelmed with a joy she didn't deserve and a peace she could never explain.

THE END

Other titles from Higher Ground Books & Media:

Wise Up to Rise Up by Rebecca Benston

A Path to Shalom by Steen Burke

For His Eyes Only by John Salmon, Ph.D.

Miracles: I Love Them by Forest Godin

Slumberland by Derra Nicole Sabo

Saved by a Mystery by Deborah Randall

Out of Darkness by Stephen Bowman

Girl's Guide to Mars by Quiaundra Nance

Of Love and Witches by Marjorie Joseph

Chronicles of a Spiritual Journey by Stephen Shepherd

My Name is Sam…And Heaven is Still Shining Through by Joe Siccardi

Add these titles to your collection today!

http://www.highergroundbooksandmedia.com

Do you have a story to tell?

Higher Ground Books & Media is an independent Christian-based publisher specializing in stories of triumph! Our purpose is to empower, inspire, and educate through the sharing of personal experiences.

Please visit our website for our submission guidelines.

http://www.highergroundbooksandmedia.com

www.ingramcontent.com/pod-product-compliance
Lightning Source LLC
Chambersburg PA
CBHW072137170626
46813CB00004BA/1603